Puck Daddy

M.A. Lee

Copyright © 2024 by M.A. Lee

All rights reserved.

No portion of this book may be reproduced in any form without written permission from the publisher or author, except as permitted by U.S. copyright law.

Contents

1. Chapter 1 — 1
2. Chapter 2 — 13
3. Chapter 3 — 24
4. Chapter 4 — 28
5. Chapter 5 — 32
6. Chapter 6 — 37
7. Chapter 7 — 49
8. Chapter 8 — 58
9. Chapter 9 — 66
10. Chapter 10 — 74
11. Chapter 11 — 80
12. Chapter 12 — 87
13. Chapter 13 — 93
14. Chapter 14 — 98

15.	Chapter 15	106
16.	Chapter 16	112
17.	Chapter 17	121
18.	Chapter 18	127
19.	Chapter 19	131
20.	Chapter 20	137
21.	Chapter 21	143
22.	Chapter 22	148
23.	Chapter 23	158
24.	Chapter 24	162
25.	Chapter 25	166
26.	Chapter 26	173
Epilogue		179
Afterword		184
About the author		186
Also by		188

Chapter 1

SAWYER

I just got hit in the face with a dildo.

Seriously, a huge dildo just flew across the store and struck me on the cheek.

"Hey, can you put that away?" I ask, watching Sadie, Skye, and Ashlynn giggle furiously.

I still don't understand how they managed to get me into a sex shop, but here I am in all its glory.

Fuck. My. Life.

"Come on, Sawyer. Have a little fun. We are in Vegas. Maybe you should buy something here in case you meet a hot guy and hook up," Skye says, winking at me. She holds out a massive vibrator and cherry-flavored lube. Easy for her to say. She's dating one of the Sunnyvale Hawks hockey players, Jace. From what I've seen between them, they are deliciously in love. Honestly, I want to die from embarrassment right now.

"Wait, I thought you were dating that guy who worked for the IT company?" Ashlynn asks, her curiosity piqued. Ashlynn attempts to keep up to date with my life, but since she started dating Logan, another Hawks hockey player, her focus has been more on her own love life than mine. Or lack thereof.

Internally groaning, I wasn't prepared for this conversation. Honestly, these girls and I really weren't friends. Ashlynn, Sadie, and I were more like co-workers since we worked in public relations or sports journalism. We all traveled to Las Vegas for work since the Hawks were in the Men's Frozen Four Tournament. I think they just felt bad that I didn't have anyone to hang out with outside of our work duties. Now, as I watch them, I realize they are interested in hearing about my sad, pathetic breakup. I had been dating Todd for about eight months before I decided to end things. At first, he was a great guy and very attentive. Then, over the last few months, something changed. He thought I worked too much and didn't make him a priority over my career. Working in public relations for the Sunnyvale University hockey team, the Hawks, keeps me busy and working long hours. I'm constantly dealing with the press, sponsors, and marketing. Not to mention, athletes who are constantly finding themselves in trouble and needing saving. I love my job and have worked hard to get where I am today. He was always jealous of me working with athletes and would make sly remarks. He always accused me of cheating, which I never would. Finally, having had enough, I broke things off right before we came to Las Vegas for the championship game. The Hawks needed me, and Todd just didn't understand that.

"No, we broke up a few days ago," I say.

"I'm sorry," Sadie offers.

"I'm not, he was a jerk. I didn't like him," Ashlynn quips.

Well, at least she's being honest.

Pushing the objects away from me, I huff as I move toward the exit of the shop. "I'm fine, we don't need to talk about it," I say.

"I know someone she wants to hook up with," Ashlynn says, giving me a knowing look. "You need a rebound."

"Ugh, I'm out of here. I will be waiting outside," I yell as I shove through the exit doors.

Once I'm outside, I feel like I can breathe. Standing on the sidewalk of the Las Vegas strip, I glance around at the crowds of people laughing and smiling.

Sometimes, I wish I could be more like my friends who are still running around the sex shop or like these people who pass me by and seem to have no cares in the world. Of course, my life isn't that easy. I work and hustle each day because nothing was ever handed to me. Everything I have, I've worked for. I'm not bitter about it, I'm just a realist. Hell, I can't even find a decent guy to date, but I chalk it up as a blessing since I really don't have time for men. Todd was the perfect example of that. Men don't understand how I can work with male athletes and not sleep with all of them.

I rubbed at my temples, feeling a headache coming on. I spent most of the day finalizing interviews with local news stations and journalists that I had talked with before we left Sunnyvale. Once we arrived, I met with four different sports podcasters who would be hosting live episodes with pre-game commentary from the players themselves and then during the game. I spoke with Sadie and other Sunnyvale journalists about the game's highlights we needed to focus on for their articles and news pieces. I was utterly exhausted and ready to fall into my comfortable hotel room bed, but the girls had other plans for me.

Sighing, I patiently wait until I see the girls walk out of the shop with bags in hand.

"Come on, Tripp just texted and said they are done with their ESPN interviews. The guys want to meet us at the rooftop restaurant of our hotel," Sadie says, showing us her cell phone.

Tripp and Sadie have been engaged for a while now and are head over heels in love. From what I understand, Tripp was the first of their friend group to fall in love. I'm still new to this group, and honestly, I'm not sure how I fit in. I work with Topher and the guys, trying to keep their images clean and present them with promotion and marketing deals. But the girls, they have their own friendships.

I met Ashlynn when her dad, the coach of the Sunnyvale Hawks, asked our PR firm to hire her. She was lost and needed some guidance. Somehow, we've developed an easygoing friendship, and she has been begging me to come out with her and the girls ever since. To my surprise, she cornered me after the game, knowing I had nowhere else to be. When she asked me to go out with them, I had no idea that meant visiting a sex shop in Las Vegas.

"Great, let's go. I'm starving," I announce to the girls.

We start walking through the crowds toward our hotel, and Ashlynn slides in next to me. "Hey, I'm sorry if we offended you," she apologizes, keeping her voice low.

Sadie and Skye are chatting up a storm behind us, and I doubt they heard her.

Guilt washes over me. They were having so much fun, and I was being a downer. "It's fine, you didn't offend me. I'm just tired. It was a long day," I say.

"Yeah, you did a great job getting press to the games," Ashlynn adds. "I'm glad you weren't too tired to come out with us." She smiles at me, and I feel that twinge of guilt again.

Shaking my head, I mustered a smile. "It was great to finally have a chance to take you up on your offer. I have to admit, it was pretty funny watching you all be cheesy back there," I giggle, pointing behind us.

Ashlynn's face lights up. "Really? I was so worried that you would think we were immature college girls. Honestly, I thought you were always blowing me off when I invited you out. Or that you were hanging out with Todd. I've never seen you go anywhere but to the office," she says, shrugging.

I respect her honesty. I've learned with Ashlynn that she doesn't hold back how she feels.

I decided I should be honest with her in return. "Since we are being truthful, I guess I was blowing you off, but not for the reasons you are thinking. I am literally married to my career. I want to move up in the company and be the head boss one day. Jodie has done a great job teaching me the ins and outs of the business. I know I need to put in extra work to make that happen. I guess I haven't left much room for fun," I admit.

It makes me sound like such a loser to say those things out loud. By the look on Ashlynn's shocked face, I guess she thinks that, too.

"You work so hard, and everyone respects and values what you do. But you still need to live a little. I mean, how are you going to meet a guy? We need to get you laid," she says way too loudly.

Skye and Sadie hustle up to us, poking their heads between me and Ashlynn.

"Oh, are we going to find Sawyer a guy?" Sadie asks, winking.

"We could hire a male prostitute. I think that's legal here," Skye adds.

A few people offer us strange glances as they pass us, having overheard our conversation.

Shaking my head, I hold up my hands. "No, that's not necessary."

"I think I know someone who would love to hook up with you," Ashlynn states proudly.

"Topher," they all say in unison.

I can feel my cheeks grow red and my panties get wet at the thought of Topher. Sure, he is undeniably gorgeous in that sexy, serious, and brooding way, but we work together. Nothing could ever happen between us.

"No, we are just friends. We work together," I attempt to argue.

The girls all roll their eyes at me as we reach our hotel. Sadie holds the door open for us, and as we slide in, we are met with the clamor of slot machines and the distant cheers from other revelers.

Thankfully, the girls leave the Topher conversation alone. After a quick stop by our hotel rooms so the girls can drop off their bags from the sex shop, we head straight to the elevator that will take us up to the rooftop. The girls check their makeup and appearances as we ride up. When the elevator doors open, we are greeted by a soft glow of string lights hanging on a gorgeous terrace. Fire-lit sconces line the walkways as a hostess escorts us to our reserved table. The guys are already seated there and when my eyes land on Topher, my heart skips a beat.

"Look, our beautiful ladies are here," Jace announces as we join the guys.

Once everyone is seated, I find myself directly across the table from Topher. The atmosphere here is romantic and breathtaking. Candles flicker in the center of the table, and the Las Vegas skyline provides the perfect backdrop for the evening.

I do my best to listen to the conversations taking place around me. Once we have all ordered, the guys begin talking about the game.

"Champions at last!" Jace bellowed, raising his glass.

Everyone cheers with him as we raise our glasses high in the air.

"Couldn't have done it without Coach Carl and Coach Topher's killer plays," Tripp states, patting Topher on the back. Coach Carl along with the rest of the coaching staff and the PR department had decided to stay in instead of celebrating like the guys are.

Watching these guys brings a smile to my face and a sense of jealousy rushing through me. They aren't just friends but family. I've watched how they look out for one another, and the love they share truly shows that blood doesn't make you family—it's the love you have for someone else.

"Time to celebrate like Vegas expects us to!" Ashlynn declares, her voice carrying above the din. "The last time I was in Las Vegas didn't—well, it didn't end so well, and we need to make up for it this time."

Logan leans over and kisses Ashlynn, whispering something in her ear that causes her to giggle. To be honest, when I first discovered Ashlynn and Logan sneaking around, I never thought they would be more than a fling. Ashlynn was the head coach's daughter, and Logan was a wild player. They surprised us all when they officially announced that they were dating. Now, they are going strong and super in love.

"Oh, we plan on enjoying our last night in Vegas," Sadie states, eyeing Tripp.

"We also need to celebrate that Sawyer is newly single," Skye adds, smiling my way.

Topher looks up from his phone and offers me a weird look. I can't tell what he's thinking, but for some reason, Skye's comment has grabbed his attention.

Our food arrives, and I dig into the sirloin steak with garlic mashed potatoes. The food is beyond divine and gives me a reason not to be so social. Truth be told, I enjoy just listening to their conversations.

Their laughter and conversation blended into the hum of the busy restaurant. Highlights from the game were the big topics of conversation, as were all of the nearby clubs the girls wanted to go to.

Drinks continued to arrive, and as I glanced around the table, I noticed that everyone was beyond tipsy.

Once everyone is finished eating, we pay our bill and then leave the restaurant. The girls have already decided which club they want to go to, and thankfully, it's in our hotel, so we don't have to go far.

"Come on, girls! This is going to be a night to remember!" Skye cheers, throwing her arms in the air, and sashays out of the restaurant.

Something tells me this is definitely going to be a night that I will never forget.

***

In the pulsating heart of the nightclub, loud music and flashing lights brought on a new kind of energy for the night. Standing next to the bar, I sipped a glass of white wine while the girls danced all over their guys. I couldn't help but notice how sexy they looked in their short, tight dresses, while I was wearing a black maxi dress. They were so carefree, dancing and singing in the middle of the dance floor. Sometimes, I wish I could be more like that.

"Sawyer, get your booty on the dance floor," Ashlynn yelled, reaching her arms out to me.

Shaking my head, I held up my glass of wine. "Maybe after I finish my drink," I yelled, but I doubt they heard me over the thumping music.

"Are you going to hide out at the bar all night?" a voice asks from behind me.

I would know that voice anywhere. Shivers race down my spine as my heart hammers in my chest.

Topher.

I turn and spot Topher leaning against the bar, those sexy eyes watching me carefully. His muscles bulge out of his light blue button-down shirt.

"Possibly," I muse. "Looks like I'm not the only one," I add, nodding his way.

Topher chuckles. Why does he have to be so damn hot? Every woman here is watching him, yet he seems oblivious to their stares.

"Yeah, a nightclub isn't really my scene, but the guys are celebrating. It's nice to see them so happy," he says, watching his friends dance with their girlfriends.

"Mine either," I agree.

We stand there watching them a little longer until Sadie runs over to us.

"Can you believe we're here?" Sadie shouted over the thumping bass. "The guys really did it! They won a championship game!"

I can't help but smile, watching her be so giddy. Normally reserved, Sadie is letting herself have fun, and I like seeing this side of her.

"Wouldn't miss it for the world!" I replied.

The rest of the crew make their way to the bar, sweating and ready for another drink.

"Guys! Guys!" Tripp's voice cut through the music as he hopped onto a nearby booth seat, commanding attention. Pulling Sadie onto the booth with him, he wraps an arm around her waist. "We've got something to tell you!" He grabs Sadie around the waist and pulls her close to his chest.

"Spill it!" Logan encouraged, wrapping an arm around Ashlynn.

"Sadie and I... We're getting married! Tonight!" Tripp announced, his grin infectious.

"Tonight?" Skye echoed, astonishment lacing her tone.

"Vegas style, baby!" Sadie squealed, bouncing on the balls of her feet.

"Wait, are you serious?" Topher asks, standing straight.

Topher is the big brother of the group and always the voice of reason. I stood next to him, just as shocked.

"Maybe you should wait until you are sober," I chime in.

"Nah, I've wanted to marry this girl since the first day I saw her," Tripp says, kissing Sadie.

"Then what are we waiting for? To the chapel!" Jace said, moving to head out of the club.

Topher and I made eye contact and we both shrugged. We could try to argue with them, but they seem so determined that I doubt our words of wisdom would help.

"Hold on, I need a shot before we go," Topher yells, causing us to stop and stare at him.

Topher orders a round of shots for the group. This isn't normal behavior for Topher. However, we all take the shots when the bartender hands them to us.

Topher stands in the middle of the group, all eyes on him. I see a glimpse of worry in Tripp's eyes, as though he worries that Topher will try and talk him out of his decision. However, Topher shocks the hell out of all of us when he raises his glass and says, "Cheers to a great night full of memories."

Placing the glass to my lips, I quickly shoot back the tequila and wince. I have no idea how I've gotten myself into this mess, but I guess I'm about to witness a wedding. Hopefully, whatever happens in Vegas stays in Vegas.

Chapter 2

TOPHER

The cool night air was refreshing after the heat of the dance floor as we spilled onto the Strip.

Did I mention that I hate clubs? Well, if I didn't before, let me make it clear now—I fucking hate clubs.

To me, a good night is watching a game, drinking an ice-cold beer, and hanging out with friends.

Not paying for over-priced drinks while drunk morons bump and grind into me.

However, after winning the Men's Frozen Four Tournament, these guys deserved to let loose and have a little fun. This was a bittersweet victory for me. Most of these guys are going pro next year, and I have interviewed for several head coaching positions. My dream would be to take over Coach Carl's spot with the Hawks. It will be sad not being with several of these guys anymore, but I'm so damn proud of them right now. Usually, I wouldn't go out with them, but none of them have the best track record when it comes to staying out of trouble, and since we are in Las Vegas—the party capital of the world—I figured it would be best for me to tag along. Plus, she would be there, too.

Sawyer.

The woman who has captured my interest since the first day I met her as Jodie's intern at the Hawks PR firm. Her sparkling blue eyes pierced right through me, and I haven't been the same since. However, no one else knows how I feel about her. Sure, the guys have given me hell when they've caught me looking at her, but I've done my best to keep everything professional with her. Right now, it's killing me to be surrounded by these couples. I stand back and watch the woman I want to nestle from afar.

The shot of tequila still burns in the back of my throat as I walk behind my drunk friends. Maybe it's the alcohol (Okay, I had one shot, but I never drink, so it's hitting me hard), but I'm feeling sentimental watching all of them in love. I've watched Tripp, Jace, and Logan grow up. Logan and I grew close as he was always getting himself into trouble. I had to focus most of my energy on him, and thankfully, he is growing out of his wild, playboy ways. I taught them everything they know about hockey and other sports. I gave them an outlet and was the one to watch out for them, because I never had that myself. We are family through and through.

Sawyer walks just in front of me, and I can sense that she is uncomfortable. She keeps tucking loose strands of her curly, blonde hair behind her ear, and those light blue eyes look nervous. My eyes keep going directly to her perfect ass. She's lean, and that figure is beyond perfect. One thing I admire most about Sawyer is that she doesn't show off her body like other girls do. She doesn't have to. Since she started working for Jodie at the PR company, I've gotten to know Sawyer. She is not only beautiful but smart and sophisticated, too. I've never met a woman like her before. I can't help but stare at her.

I see a sign for the little White Chapel ahead, and we all head that way. I can't believe they want to get married. Tripp is about to head off to the NHL, and Sadie will be an influential writer one day. They have the makings of a power couple, but marriage—that just seems intense at their age.

We all stumbled into the chapel. I notice the cheesy dresses and tuxes to my right and pictures of happy couples getting married to my left. Straight ahead is a long aisle that leads to an altar with a flower arch.

"Are we really doing this?" Sadie laughs, pulling me out of my trance.

"Of course we are. Not getting cold feet, are you?" Tripp asks, holding her tightly.

I want to poke fun at Tripp right now, but I don't dare ruin his happiness. The guy has come a long way, and it makes me glad to see him so happy and in love. Sadie is a great girl, and I couldn't pick a better partner for him.

"We are going to be bridesmaids!" Ashlynn cheers, tugging the girls to follow her.

A man in a black suit walks down the aisle toward us. "Can I help you?"

"We are here to get married," Tripp tells him, smiling.

The man in the suit begins explaining what they need to do, including packages they can purchase to remember their big day. I stand back, taking it all in. Logan hands me another shot, and I turn to him.

"Where did you get this?" I ask, taking the shot. Glancing around, I notice Ashlynn is handing everyone in our group shots.

"The chapel has a bar," Logan says, pointing to a small bar area next to the dresses and tuxedos. Of course a wedding chapel in Las Vegas would have a bar, too.

Sawyer stands next to me, shot in hand. We watch everyone move toward the altar. Sadie is now wearing a veil, and Skye hands her a bouquet of fake flowers.

"Are we seriously going to let them do this?" Sawyer asks, her blue eyes staring at me.

"I think they have their hearts set on this. If they wake up tomorrow and regret it, then they can have a do-over. They are engaged," I explain.

Sawyer nods. There is a sadness in her expression that I can't read. My hands twitch at my sides to touch her. The urge to kiss her is so strong that I take a step back to put distance between us.

"Yeah, I know what you are saying. It must be nice to be so in love that you would throw caution to the wind and get married on a whim," Sawyer says with a sigh.

Her words strike me. Sawyer could have any man she wants. She's probably got a trail of broken hearts behind her. That douchebag, Todd, being one of them. I was happy to hear they broke up, but I know not to make a move right now. We work together, and I have to keep my feelings for her locked away.

"Come on guys, we are about to start the ceremony," Skye yells.

Turning to Sawyer, I hold out the shot glass. "Cheers to the happy couple," I say.

We clink glasses and throw back the shots. We prepare ourselves to watch Tripp and Sadie get married. Standing in the back of the chapel, I watch my best friend get married as I stand next to a woman I love but can't have.

***

An hour later, we are celebrating the newly married couple at yet another loud bar.

My head is spinning from all of the shots we've been taking. Even Sawyer is smiling and laughing as she holds a margarita in her hand, giggling with the girls.

Everyone seems to be having a great time, and Sadie and Tripp can't seem to keep their hands off one another.

"Hey, I'm taking my bride back to our room to consummate our marriage," Tripp yells over the loud music and voices.

"Gross," I say, smiling.

We all offer one last shout of "Congratulations" as the married couple leaves the bar. I wonder if they will even make it back to their room before they decide to get down and dirty.

Logan and Ashlynn move back to the dance floor followed by Skye and Jace. They kiss and touch as they forget about the rest of the world around them. As happy as I am for my friends, it stings standing on the sidelines while everyone around me gets their happily ever after. Don't get me wrong. I'm not miserable in my life. I've worked hard to become a coach for the Sunnyvale Hawks. I love the life I've created. I even bought a house. But knowing that I can't have the one woman I want to spend my life with—makes nights like this harder.

"Well, I'm drunk and ready to leave," Sawyer sighs next to me.

I see the longing in her eyes as she watches the couples dance. Sawyer is strong, but I spy glimpses of sadness in her.

"Me, too," I agree with her.

I push off the bar and stumble a little. I guess I'm more drunk than I thought. Sawyer giggles as she watches me attempt to right myself.

"I think you are drunk," she points out, sliding off the barstool. When her feet touch the floor, she wobbles and grabs hold of the bar to keep herself from falling.

Laughing, I reached my hand out to her. "I think we are both a little drunk," I offer.

"Maybe we can help each other. We just need to get back to our hotel. I think it's over there." Sawyer attempts to point, but she spins, and I catch her, pulling her into my arms.

For a brief moment, our eyes lock, and I notice my lips are only inches away from hers. Those big blue eyes stare up at me, and I pull away before I do something dumb and kiss her.

Helping her stand, I lock my arm through hers. "Alright, let's see if we can figure out how to get back to our rooms."

Once again, we leave a dark club and enter the neon splendor of the Las Vegas Strip. It's like an entirely different world out here. The air was thick with the scent of possibility, or maybe that was just the buzz of alcohol that made everything seem more vibrant.

Stumbling down the sidewalk, Sawyer begins to giggle. "I got hit in the face by a dildo today," she says way too loudly.

This causes me to stop and belt out a huge laugh. A guy in front of us stops and turns, giving Sawyer a weird glance. "Did you see that guy's face when you—" I begin, but my words dissolve into another fit of laughter as I watch Sawyer's face beam.

I've never seen her so carefree and lighthearted.

"Priceless!" Sawyer managed to say, her long blonde hair catching the flashing lights as she threw her head back gleefully. "Hey! Look, another little chapel!" she yells in my ear, pointing down the street.

Somehow, we got ourselves turned around and walked several blocks toward the old part of Las Vegas, back to where Tripp and Sadie got married.

"That one looks like the one Britney Spears got married in," she laughs, trying to do a little dance.

"Well, we should go check it out. I bet they have a bar, too," I say, taking her hand and leading her toward the little white building.

Something in my mind tells me we should be going somewhere else, but I've forgotten where. We enter the little building and are once again greeted by shots of alcohol and fun costumes to try on. We laugh and carry on, even walking down the aisle and pretending to get married. I even get to kiss the bride!

Once Sawyer has seen enough, she announces that she needs to get back to the hotel. Just as quickly as we entered this place, we are now departing.

"That was fun," I slur, twirling Sawyer around. She stumbles slightly, her heels uneven against the pavement. Holding her in my arms feels like heaven, and I don't want to let her go.

"Wow, I think we are super drunk," she says, but the words come out garbled.

"Whoa there. Let me hold you until we get inside," I say, spotting our hotel.

"Ha, you're hilarious," she shoots back, her wit as quick as ever. "But for the record, I am perfectly capable—"

"Of walking in a straight line? Yeah, I've seen toddlers on skates have better balance than you do right now," I teased, guiding her toward the grand entrance of our hotel.

"Shut up, Coach," she retorted, but there was warmth in her voice that caused my dick to stir.

Once inside our hotel, I led us to the elevators. As the doors slid open, I pulled Sawyer inside. She stands close to me, even though we are the only two in the elevator. I've fantasized so many times about having Sawyer in my arms, near me. My hands lingered on her waist, and Sawyer didn't move away.

"Topher..." she began, unsure what she intended to say. Her blue eyes pierced my soul. There was an intensity in how she said my name that made my breath falter.

"Sawyer," I interrupted, my voice suddenly serious.

As I looked down at this beautiful woman, my eyes searching hers, I could feel the spark between us.

Leaning down, my lips hovered inches above hers. My head swam, and we were both unsteady, but I knew that there was no backing down now.

"Sawyer, I want to—" my words trailed off as my lips touched hers. I was crossing a line. I knew I should have stopped, but I couldn't. Those plump lips were soft and smooth like silk. I wanted more.

A slight moan escaped her lips, and that was all it took for me to kiss her even harder. My hands went to her soft hair, pulling her closer to me. Her hands wrapped around me, reaching the nape of my neck, and her body molded into mine. Even in my drunken stupor, I knew that I was kissing Sawyer, and nothing would ever be the same again.

The elevator dinged, breaking the spell just enough for us to part breathlessly. When she looked at me, I knew that I couldn't walk away now. Exiting onto our floor, the tension was beyond electric. Leading us down the hallway, Sawyer stopped when we reached my room. It was now or never. I would never push her to do something that she didn't want to do. My mind hazy, I clumsily pulled my key card out of my pocket and swiped it, unlocking the room. Opening the door, I glanced at Sawyer.

Hesitating, she bit her lip as she stood, one hand leaning on the doorframe. Suddenly, she rushed forward, wrapping her arms around my neck, and crushed her lips against mine. Stumbling into my room, I kicked the door closed as I lifted her into my arms, my hands cupping her perfectly round ass. Hearing the door close behind us, all thoughts of the outside world fell away.

"Are you sure about this?" I asked, pulling away from her momentarily. Drunk or not, I had to know that she was fully aware of what we were about to do.

"What happens when we get back to Sunnyvale?" she breathes. "This could change everything."

I see the turmoil in her eyes. I want this more than anything, and my drunk brain has forgotten all the reasons why this is a bad idea.

"Do you want to do this?" I ask.

"Yes," she breathed.

As I stared into her eyes, I walked us to the bed and lay her down. Climbing over her body, our kisses became a tangle of touching and biting. Her skin tasted sweet, and I couldn't get enough of her. All I could think about was that I finally had Sawyer in my arms.

"Let's just live in the here and now," I say, and went back to kissing her.

Her skin was so smooth as I trailed kisses down her neck. My hands slipped under her dress, and I felt how wet she was for me when my fingers traced over her panties. Her hands were tugging at my shirt, so we broke apart, allowing me to pull my shirt off. As our clothes were ripped away, all I could think about was that I finally had Sawyer. Everything about her was beyond incredible. Cupping her breast, I rolled my tongue over her sensitive nipple, eliciting another moan from her.

"That feels good," she said, her words sounding satisfied.

Arching her back, she pushed herself closer to me. Her body was screaming for me to continue kissing and touching. And that is exactly what I plan to do all night. Worshiping this woman is all I've ever wanted.

I just hoped I would remember this night when we both sobered up.

Chapter 3

SAWYER

I woke to my alarm wailing.

Rolling over, I reached for my phone on the hotel room nightstand, only to discover that instead of touching a table, my hand encountered a body. Shooting up, I instantly regretted the quick movement. A searing pain shoots through my head as my stomach begins to churn. I spot my phone on the floor, and, to my horror, it's next to my dress.

What in the hell? Why am I not in my hotel room?

Glancing around, I rub my eyes as I struggle to recall the events of the night before.

Jumping out of bed, I grabbed my phone off the floor and turned off the alarm. My head swims, and I fight down the vomit racing up my throat. As I turn, I spot Topher lying in bed. One arm is draped over the side of the bed and the other rests under a sheet that barely covers his naked body. Damn, how can a man look that glorious and sexy while sleeping? His toned abs show off the hours he spends working out and skating with his team. His light snores are cute. Focus, Sawyer. Think back to last night.

Suddenly, flashes of too many tequila shots, a wedding chapel, and Topher kissing me race through my mind. Freezing in place, I am shocked as I realize what I have done.

I had sex with Topher last night.

Several times.

I reach for my dress, panties, and bra and quickly dress. I have to get the hell out of here. I will face the consequences of my actions once I get back to Sunnyvale. But for now, I need to sneak out of this room.

Scurrying toward the door, I hit my knee against the bathroom doorframe and cringed. Slowly, I turned my head. Thankfully, Topher is still sound asleep. My heart breaks as I realize I'm leaving without talking to him about... whatever this was.

A one-night stand?

A drunken mistake?

Tears begin to fill my eyes, and I take a deep breath and open the door. Escaping into the hall, I glance back one last time to see Topher's sweet face. I just hope he can forgive me.

***

"Where are you?"

Sitting in the airport, I finally mustered the courage to go through my texts and missed calls. Ashlynn called me four times this morning, and I realized I needed to answer.

"Hey, I'm at the airport," I say, watching the screen in front of me display boarding times. I have five minutes until I can get on the airplane returning to Sunnyvale.

"What?" she screeches, causing me to hold the phone away from my ear. "Why are you at the airport? We weren't leaving until tonight." I can hear the disappointment in her tone, and I feel bad.

"Sorry. I have so much work to do, so I decided to head back home early," I told her.

It's not necessarily a lie, but it's totally not the whole truth either. I can't begin to explain to her how badly I screwed up last night. I never get drunk, and this is exactly why. Apparently, I make terrible decisions when I drink.

Like sleeping with Topher.

"Okay," she says, and I hear the disappointment in her tone. "We need to catch up when we are all back in town. Oh, have you talked to Topher today?"

"No, why would I?" I shoot out. Instantly, I regret sounding so guilty.

"No reason. The guys haven't been able to get ahold of him. Well, have a safe flight," she finishes.

Once we hang up, I text Jodie to let her know that I will be back in the office early. I'm sure she will want to jump on some new marketing ideas for the guys, and sponsors will want to meet with them, too. When I finally board the plane, I close my eyes and pray that my hangover subsides by the time I arrive back in Sunnyvale.

Chapter 4

Topher

Fuck. My. Life.

What the hell is that pounding noise? And why do I feel like I've been hit by a freight truck/train? Groaning, I roll over and check the time. It's past four in the afternoon, and I'm still sleeping.

"Topher, are you in there? Open up!" I hear Jace yell outside of my hotel room.

Sitting up, I rub my hands over my face. "Hold on!" I call back.

Why do I feel like death right now? Closing my eyes, I struggle to think back to last night.

"Topher, we are just checking to see if you are alive," Logan states. His voice is muffled through the door, and I can hear Jace chuckle.

"I'm alive. I will call you all when I'm up. Leave me alone," I roar.

I can hear them laughing as they move down the hallway. Falling back onto the bed, I am instantly met with a sweet lavender scent that only one woman I know wears.

Sawyer.

I would recognize that scent anywhere. I chase it each day at the arena. Inhaling deeply, I close my eyes as flashes of last night hit me. Somehow, I ended up alone with Sawyer. More shots, and we had sex. Damn, I hooked up with her last night, and I only have drunken images in my mind to remind me. Somehow, that is worse than the raging hangover I'm sporting right now.

Thinking of Sawyer, I realize the hotel room is silent.

"Sawyer," I call out, but I'm only met with stillness.

Her clothes aren't here, and she is nowhere in sight. Grabbing my phone off the floor, I see a million texts from the guys. I don't know how I allowed myself to get so drunk. I need to talk to Sawyer. I go to find her number in my phone when a link from an unknown number appears.

Oh great, what is this? Clicking the link, I fall back onto the bed as images of Sawyer and me walking down an aisle come on the screen.

We are smiling, laughing, and stumbling as we hold onto one another. The sad part is we look happy. Like, really happy. Maybe the happiest I've ever seen both of us.

I continue watching, my stomach begins to drop as I hear an Elvis impersonator announce us as husband and wife. I kiss Sawyer, and when she looks at me, it almost makes me believe she has true feelings for me. But I know that can't be the truth. That's just my mind and alcohol playing tricks on my heart.

This is bad. So, so bad.

Closing the link, I throw my phone on the bed. What the hell am I going to do? Not only did I have sex with Sawyer, but we got married, too? And now, I have no idea where she is.

Forcing myself up again, I grab my phone a second time and find her number. The call goes straight to voicemail, so I decide to leave a text.

Me: Hey, I'm sorry I missed you this morning. When I get back into town, can we talk?

I hit send before I can stop myself. Does she know what we did last night? Rubbing a hand over my jaw, I try to think back to any conversations we could have had. All I remember is laughing and kissing—lots of kissing.

Another thought pops into my head, and I text the guys in our group chat.

Me: Did any of you see me and Sawyer after we left Tripp and Sadie's wedding?

I sit back and watch the little bubbles dance across the screen as they are each typing something.

Logan: No. Ashlynn said Sawyer wasn't really in the mood to party, so she guessed she went back to the hotel. I assumed the same for you. Why?

Jace: No, I was black-out drunk. I don't even remember how I got back to the hotel. You ok, man?

Tripp: I was too busy having sex with my wife on every surface of our hotel room to care what you shitheads were doing.

Groaning, I have an urge to hit something. Thankfully, they have no idea what Sawyer and I did last night. Still, I'm worried that Sawyer knows and is too upset to talk with me. Or worse, she is oblivious to the fact that we are now husband and wife.

Deciding I can't hide out in my room all day, I rush into the bathroom and shower. I have an interview today that Sawyer set up with some Sports Center journalists, and Coach Carl wants me there early. I look and feel like shit. Like it or not, finding out what is really going on with Sawyer and I will have to wait until I get back to Sunnyvale.

Chapter 5

SAWYER

Nursing a very strong coffee, I sit at my desk staring at my calendar.

"Earth to Sawyer," Jodie sings, knocking on my open office door. Startled, I almost choked on my coffee. Laughing, she walks into my office. "Sorry, didn't mean to scare you."

Looking poised and regal as always, Jodie wears a black pencil skirt and silver blouse. Her hair is in a tight updo, and she wears pearls that shine against the light in the room.

Waving for her to sit in one of the office chairs facing my desk, I do my best to look upbeat. "It's okay. I was just reviewing my calendar," I say, pointing to my computer screen.

"I didn't expect to see you back in the office today." Jodie pins me with a pointed look.

When she sent me to Las Vegas with the team, she had warned me not to return early. She stated I needed to live a little and enjoy my time away from Sunnyvale. Jodie has been more than my boss and mentor; she's also been a friend and confidant. I didn't have many friends growing up in Los Angeles. When I moved to Sunnyvale to attend college and started my internship with Jodie, she had been the only person to truly believe in me. She knows how I'm at the office most days before the sun rises and that I don't leave until dark.

I offer a smile, knowing I'm about to get a lecture.

"Well, I needed to get started on some things," I attempt to argue.

Rolling her eyes, Jodie laughs. "Sure, we will talk about that later. So, how was Las Vegas? Did you see any shows? Gamble? Go out and make terrible decisions?"

I feel my face warm as thoughts rush to Topher. I still have his text on my phone and haven't had the courage to respond. Having a talk after the night we had won't be easy. Maybe if I ignore it, all of this will go away.

Sitting up straighter, Jodie places her hands on my desk. "I see your cheeks growing red. So, which one was it? Let me guess, all three!"

This time, I laugh. "Doubtful. I went out one night with the girls and left early after Tripp and Sadie got married," I announce.

"What? Married?" Jodie squeals, jumping out of the chair.

BINGO! I knew that little tidbit of information would make her forget about me. One of her star hockey players getting married in Vegas would be big on social media and news outlets once people found out.

"Oh yeah, you didn't know?" I ask coyly.

Furiously shaking her head, Jodie begins to rush toward the door. "I need to call Tripp. Why didn't anyone tell me about this? We need to get a statement out to the press. I need to call Tripp and Sadie. I'm going to ring their necks," she says, running down the hallway.

A part of me feels guilty for outing Tripp and Sadie to save my own ass, but a girl has to do what a girl has to do. Left alone, I go back to staring at my computer. I spend the next few hours answering emails and working on our social media accounts. With a big win for the Hawks, I need to ensure the guys get more sponsorships and those wanting to go pro get their agents working on marketing. I make sure to stay hidden away in my office, so I don't run into anyone else for the rest of the day.

Especially Topher.

***

It's been three days since I've been back in Sunnyvale.

Of course, Jodie jumped right into damage control mode once pictures and information leaked from Tripp and Sadie's Vegas wedding. As for me, I've done my best to hide from the team, but today, I have to attend a meeting with the entire team and coaching staff.

I've been a nervous wreck all morning. I shouldn't be afraid to see Topher, but I am. I've been dodging his calls and texts.

Walking down the hall, I enter the large conference room where we hold all of our meetings. It's large enough to hold the team, coaches, agents, the PR team, and any media that gets invited. I slide into the room as people are chatting with one another. The room is buzzing with excitement from the recent win.

Finding a seat in the back, I sit in one of the black leather chairs that faces the front of the room. The entire space is equipped with four large oak tables, a television screen the size of an entire wall, and a large buffet area with catered food for everyone to enjoy. With my eyes trained on my phone, I do my best not to look around, but I feel his eyes on me the moment he enters the room.

Hesitating, I finally managed to glance up and spot Topher staring at me from across the room. Those dark eyes bore into me, and his jaw was tense from scowling. When our eyes meet, I feel heat pour through my body. Flashes of his lips covering my skin and his hands tangled in my hair make me squirm in my seat. This is exactly why I have been avoiding him. Seeing him before our hook up was difficult, but I always managed to keep my emotions in check. Now, knowing what those hands can do… I don't know how I will ever look at him again.

Thankfully, Coach Carl enters the room, and everyone goes quiet. All eyes are trained on him. I use him as an excuse to look away from Topher. I know that eventually, he will catch up with me, but for now, I will hide away like the chicken-shit that I am.

"Thank you all for being here with me this morning as we celebrate the Men's Frozen Four Champions!" Coach Carl bellows, and the room erupts in cheers and fist bumps. I smile, watching the excitement build. Holding his arms out, Coach Carl motions for everyone to settle down.

"Now that we have a championship title, our work is just starting. We have a few guys leaving us for the NHL, and those announcements will be made next week. I'm sad to see them go, but I can't wait to cheer them on in the big leagues." He pauses and looks toward Tripp, Jace, Logan, and three other senior players. I already knew they were going pro, but it's still great to hear it being shared. "But that's not why we are here today. They will get their moment to shine. Right now, I have a very important announcement to make." The room stills as he grows more serious. I look at Jodie, and she nods. Coach Carl had mentioned to us a month ago that he was ready to retire. This must be his retirement announcement before we take it public.

"I have been honored to be your coach over the last few years. As much as I've loved my time at Sunnyvale, I have decided it's time for me to step down and retire." A few guys groan and look around the room. I can tell this is difficult news for them. "I wanted to be the first to tell you who my replacement would be." At this, Topher stands and walks to the front of the room to stand next to Coach Carl. As people notice, I hear clapping and shouts from across the room. "I want you all to welcome the new Sunnyvale Hawks Hockey Team's newest head coach, Topher Lewis."

As the room erupts all around me, all I can do is stare at Topher, who has his eyes trained right on me.

Chapter 6

TOPHER

"Congratulations!"

The cheers poured out of the team as Coach Carl announces I'm the new coach. After our championship win, Coach Carl called me and told me he was ready to retire. With Ashlynn and Logan engaged, he wanted to spend more time with his family and make up for lost time. I don't exactly get it, but I respect him even more for choosing his family over his career. Obviously, I was more than happy to accept his offer. Ever since I stepped foot on Sunnyvale's campus, it has been my dream to be a head coach for the Hawks. I had interviewed with a couple of other teams, but I had my heart set on Sunnyvale.

Now, as I should be living in the moment when my dream is finally coming true, I can't stop thinking about Sawyer. More beautiful than ever, she sits in the back of the room, watching me with hazy eyes. I feel an urgency to cross this room and go to her, but I compose myself and stand in place. As crazy as it seems, I realize that I've missed her. Normally, we see each other throughout our day at the arena. Harmless flirting and work conversations fill our time. She's been avoiding me since I got back into town, and I know it. Once this meeting is over, I'm going to force her to talk to me whether she likes it or not.

"Topher, would you like to say anything?" Coach Carl asks.

I'm pulled from my Sawyer-filled haze/trance as I remember why I am here. I remove my eyes from Sawyer and look out at the guys who entrusted their college hockey careers to my hands. Then, I looked toward Tripp, Logan, and Jace. They have always trusted me, following me to Sunnyvale and taking the advice I gave them, which led to them becoming elite players who will go pro next year. Now, I get to be the head coach and lead the team to more championships.

"Let's hear it, coach," Phoenix yells from near the window. He's a rookie who has a ton of potential along with a big ego.

Smiling, I begin. "I want to thank Coach Carl, Sunnyvale University, and the rest of you for trusting me to be your new coach. I'm excited to see where we lead the Hawks next season," I say, pumping my fist in the air.

Everyone jumps up, yelling congratulations and shaking my hand. This is surreal to me—an honest dream come true—but my mind is spinning as I watch Sawyer slink out the door.

"Topher, can I have a word with you?" Coach Carl asks.

"Sure," I agree. This man was my mentor and idol for years. I would do anything for him.

We walked down the hallways to his old office. It's strange to think this will all be mine. Most of his personal items have already been cleared out, but there is still so much of him lingering in here.

"Topher, I'm really proud of you," Coach Carl says.

I'm taken aback. Coach Carl isn't an emotional man and rarely gives out compliments. "Thanks," I manage.

"I wanted to let you know that several sports agents have reached out to me. They want to represent several of the seniors, especially Tripp, Jace, and Logan. This is big for them. I've also had many NHL teams asking about the guys. I think they will all go pro when they graduate in the spring."

Hearing him say this warms my heart. I've coached Tripp, Jace, and Logan since they were kids. This was our ultimate end goal—to get them to the pros. I know a couple of the guys want to coach like me or be sports broadcasters, but this is their ticket. All of our hard work is finally paying off.

"That's so great. They all deserve everything that's coming their way," I agree with him.

"I wanted you to have the honor of telling Tripp, Jace, and Logan that the new NHL team being created right outside of Sunnyvale is prepared to offer all three of them contracts. They need to get signed on with agents first, but you should be the one to tell them," he informs me.

"It would be my pleasure," I tell him.

I shake his hand, grateful for the man standing in front of me who helped me get to this point in my career. I'm elated, but in the back of my mind, I know there is another pressing matter that takes precedence right now. I will get with the guys as soon as I talk to Sawyer.

Twenty minutes later, I finally escape the conference room and head straight to Sawyer's office. I had planned on going to find Sawyer as soon as the conference ended, but I was stopped by guys on the team who wanted to congratulate me. I did my best to appease them, while still trying to rush out of there. Once I make it to the PR floor, I'm a man on a mission and know this is the perfect time to catch her. She probably assumes I will be caught up with answering questions and talking to the guys, so I won't come looking for her.

I spot Sawyer in her office, sitting with her back to me as she stares down at the ice below. I've always loved how their offices have the perfect view of the rink. Clearing my throat, I don't bother knocking on the door. I think we have moved past pleasantries.

Hearing me, Sawyer spins in her leather chair. I see her face is red, and she's wiping tears away from her eyes.

"Hey, what's wrong?" I asked, rushing to her side.

She stiffens as I get near, and that causes me to halt in my tracks. "Topher, what are you doing here?"

I'm caught off guard by her disheveled appearance and clipped tone. "I have been trying to talk to you for days," I state.

She shakes her head and looks away for a moment. "Topher, I've been meaning to get back to you, but I've been busy," she begins. "The press got word of Tripp's Vegas wedding, and it's been crazy around here."

I know that part is true. I've seen the videos and photos on social media and sports channels. Tripp doesn't seem to care, but the team is trying to make sure this doesn't hurt his image or chances with his new team.

"Sawyer, don't lie to me. We need to talk about what happened in…"

Before I can finish my sentence, Sawyer jumps from her chair, races behind me, and closes her office door.

"Someone could hear you," she shushes me.

For some reason, her fear of someone hearing about us sends fire searing through me. I'm hurt, and there's no other way to feel. The woman I've wanted for so long seems almost embarrassed about me.

"Are you really going to be like this? We have been friends and colleagues for a long time. What happened was fun and amazing," I say, allowing my feelings to finally be exposed. I have to be vulnerable with her right now. This is my only chance to shoot my shot.

Sawyer leans against the closed door, and my eyes travel down her body. She's wearing black dress pants that hug her curves and make her ass look appetizing. The red silk shirt she wears makes her tits pop and reminds me of how soft her skin feels.

"Topher, we were so drunk. I don't even really remember that night," she breathed.

I rub at my temples. Why is she being so infuriating? "What do you remember?" I question.

She thinks for a moment, biting her lip in worry. It's so damn sexy. "I remember lots of shots and then waking up naked in your bed. Other than that, most of it is a blur," she sighs.

I watch her closely, looking for more signs that she remembers anything. I feel like she's holding something back, but I don't think pushing her for more information is going to help.

"Yeah, I remember that and something else," I begin, pulling my phone out of my pocket and opening the link to the video I was sent. Turns out it was from the owner of the chapel where we got married.

I move to stand in front of Sawyer, and when she looks at my screen, I see the horror etched in her features. Her hands move to her mouth, and she gasps. "What is this?" she cries.

When the video ends, I stuff my phone back in my pocket. "Apparently, we got married, too," I explain.

A fury erupts inside of her as she pushes herself off the door and gets in my face. "Why didn't you tell me!? This is so bad. We are married!" She starts pacing around the room, huffing and puffing.

"I tried to tell you, but you've been ghosting me!" I yell.

She stops and spins in her black Stiletto heels. "We have to get this annulled. No one can know about this," she says, this time her tone is softer but sad.

It breaks my heart to see her like this. "Sawyer, we can figure something out. Just talk to me," I plead with her.

Moving to her desk, Sawyer falls into her chair. I stand in the center of the room and give her a moment to compose herself. Finally, I break the silence. "Sawyer, there has been chemistry between us for a while. You and I both know it. What happened in Las Vegas was because we both wanted it to happen. I know we rushed through everything, but maybe if we give this a chance, it could be great." I'm pouring my heart out to her, praying that she hears me. I know she has had a crush on me, too. I've seen her watching me.

"Topher, you don't understand," she whispers.

"Make me understand," I say, moving to kneel in front of her.

She sighs. "I have worked really hard to get where I am with my career, and you have too. We can't have a scandal ruining anything. You are the head coach now. I have dreams. Maybe if it were years down the road, we could make this work, but right now, I don't have time for a relationship." She looks up at me, tears brimming in those beautiful eyes.

My heart shatters in my chest. I want to beg her to change her mind, but I also have to respect what she is saying. Sawyer works harder than anyone I've ever met. I wish things were different, but they aren't.

"Not even a husband?" I chuckled.

For the first time since I arrived in her office, she smiles. "Definitely not a husband," she laughs. "I'm so sorry."

"Me, too. But I understand. I will find an attorney who can annul this. I promise I will take care of it," I swear to her.

Once again, my heart shatters into a million fucking pieces. I can't believe this is all happening.

"Can we just go back to being friends?" she asks as I hesitate in the doorway.

One last final blow to my already wounded ego and soul. "Of course. Friends," I say, slipping out of her office.

***

"Hey, open up!" a voice yells from my front porch.

I'm standing in my kitchen, staring inside my empty refrigerator, when a pounding on my front door causes me to jump.

"I've got cold beer and pizza!" Jace shouts.

Shaking my head, I close the refrigerator and move to the front door. All I wanted was a quiet evening where I could stew in my self-pity after being friend-zoned, once again, by Sawyer.

Opening the door, I'm greeted by Logan, Jace, and Tripp standing on my small front porch.

"Welcome to the bachelor pad," I announced, opening the door wider.

The guys walk past me into the sparsely decorated living room. An old leather couch that had seen better days is positioned strategically in front of a television set. I should have purchased more furniture by now, but it hasn't been a priority.

"Yeah, we've been waiting for our formal invite," Jace states, placing a case of beer and a pizza box on my kitchen counter.

Tripp pats me on the shoulder as he grabs a beer for himself. "I just got back from my honeymoon. Thought we would come over and celebrate your new coaching position," he announces. "Sadie and the girls are having a spa day, so I've got a few hours to hang with you."

Laughing, I reach for a beer and crack open the pizza box. The smell of cheese and pepperoni pizza makes my mouth water. Beer and greasy food are just what I need .

"Honeymoon?" I cock an eyebrow.

"Yeah, I spent two days in Malibu with Sadie. Two glorious days of just us," he says proudly.

"I still can't believe you are married," Jace chimes in, shaking his head.

"Me either. I'm proud of you," Logan announces. Our banter is easy, but clearly, we are all proud of Tripp.

I'm in awe of the man Tripp has become. I used to worry that he would somehow ruin his chances at remaining on his athletic scholarship, but he has pleasantly surprised me. He's become a great guy and now—a husband.

We move to the living room, and everyone starts looking around for seating. I moved to the small leather recliner that I bought a few years ago. As we sit, Sports Center hums in the background.

"Man, you weren't kidding about needing a decorator," Jace chuckled, looking around.

"I'll get to it," I say.

"Who needs decorations when you've got the essentials?" Logan retorted, making a beeline for the couch, his athletic build sinking into the cushions as he snatched up the remote. "Sports Center and pizza. It's all good."

"So, who is getting married next?" I ask, turning the attention back on the guys.

Jace and Logan smirk while Tripp watches them squirm.

"I wouldn't be opposed to it one day," Logan quips.

"Me either, but I need to make sure I get my degree first," Jace adds.

"Damn, when did you all grow up on me?" I chuckled.

"Hey, who says we are grown up?" Jace argues, smiling.

"Seriously, Topher, congrats on the head coach gig," Jace said, clapping me on the back with a broad smile. His warm brown eyes mirrored the sentiment. "Sunnyvale Hawks are lucky to have you."

"Thanks, man." I hated all of the congratulations I was hearing. It felt good, but these guys didn't need to do this for me. I owe them just as much as they owe me. "Wouldn't have made it here without you guys having my back all of these years."

"Ah, come on. You're the one with the killer strategies," Jace interjected, grabbing a slice of pepperoni pizza from the box on the coffee table, his wit shining through as usual. "We just showed up for the free food."

"Speaking of which," Logan added, snagging his own piece, "this is great and all, but when's the housewarming party? You know, with actual people? We've waited years for you to get your own place so we could throw killer parties."

This caused me to laugh and think back to when I was in high school, and they were still in middle school. They would follow me around, hoping to get a few minutes to hang out with my friends or get invited to a party. Turns out, not much has changed.

"Let's not scare him off with social interactions just yet," Jace teased, glancing over at me with an amused smirk.

"Hey, I can be social," I protested. "Right now, I'm focused on the team. We've got a lot of work ahead."

"I was shocked when he agreed to go out with us in Vegas," Tripp mused.

My thoughts went back to that night in Vegas, and my mood instantly dropped as Sawyer's beautiful face came to mind.

"Always the serious one," Logan noted, shaking his head but smiling, nonetheless. "No doubt you'll whip them into shape."

"Damn right," Jace asserted, his muscular frame tensing with determination. "The Hawks are gonna soar this season, just watch. Hey, one of us has to be responsible. Turns out, it's just always been Topher."

Yeah, I've always been responsible...

If they only knew what really happened in Vegas, I wonder if they would still look at me the same way.

Chapter 7

SAWYER

It's been four weeks since I discovered that Topher and I accidentally got married and hooked up in Las Vegas.

I wish I could say that things had returned to normal, but that isn't the case. In fact, things have been awkward.

As promised, Topher contacted an attorney to help us get an annulment, but we were at a standstill due to both of us being incredibly busy at work. For now, we were pretending like that night never happened, so I wasn't going to rush the process.

Work had been hectic since the news of Topher becoming the new head coach had been released to the press. Add in the recent championship, and everyone seemed to want a piece of the Hawks.

Jodie comes sweeping into my office, her cell phone tucked against her ear as she falls into the chair in front of my desk. I watch her with a smile as I pop another Rolaid in my mouth. I must have caught a stomach bug. I haven't been feeling the best lately. Maybe I'm just exhausted from all of the work.

Jodie ends the call and blows out a heavy breath. "That was another sponsor," she says, her smile widening.

"That's great! These guys are going to be very busy in the off-season," I say.

Right after the championship win, Tripp, Jace, and Logan all signed on with agents and offered contracts to play for a new NHL team. We've had sponsors begging them to endorse their products before they hit it big. It's a brave choice to go with a new pro team, but I think it's an excellent opportunity for the guys to create something great. That's what Topher did when he first came to Sunnyvale. And just like that, my thoughts are back on Topher.

"Well, this one was for Topher. You know that new car dealership in Sunnyvale?" she asks.

"Yeah, I've seen their commercials."

"They want Topher to come and promote some of their cars. They even want to give him one to drive!" She claps her hands at this.

"Wow, that's great!" Even though things between me and Topher have been awkward, I'm still so happy for him. I spent a lot of time researching the Hawks before starting my internship. Topher began his career at Sunnyvale as a hockey player. The program was just starting, and no one believed that a small beach college in California could have a successful hockey team. Once they started winning games and tournaments, people noticed them. Add in Topher recruiting Tripp, Jace, and Logan, and the team has been winning and gaining sponsors. Sunnyvale University is now getting donors to the school and putting its name in the sports world. Topher deserves this, and I'm truly happy for him.

"I gave them your contact information. They want to schedule a commercial shoot next week, and I need you to be there to help supervise."

"Sounds good," I say, my stomach grumbling loudly.

"Also, the university is hosting a formal party to welcome Topher as the new coach. It's this Friday evening from six to nine. We will need to be in attendance." As she explains this, my stomach drops, and I feel like I'm going to vomit.

"Okay, sure. No problem."

Noticing my change in mood, Jodie raises her eyes. "Hey, are you okay? You don't look so good. Your face is really pale all of a sudden."

Throwing my hand to my mouth, I stand and rush out of the room toward the restroom. I make it just in time to watch my breakfast go straight into the toilet. Once I'm finished, I wash my face and mouth in the sink and head back to my office. I don't feel great, but at least my stomach seems more settled.

Jodie is still sitting in my office, watching me like I've grown two heads. "Maybe you need to go home," Jodie advises.

Shaking my head, I move back to my desk. "No, I will finish up today. If I feel bad tomorrow, I will work from home," I offer.

Pursing her lips, I can see that Jodie wants to argue, but thankfully, she doesn't. She knows me all too well, and I'm too stubborn to go home. "Fine, but promise me that if you get sick again, you will go home," she states, standing and moving to leave my office.

Once she's gone, I stand by my desk and compose myself. I have so much work to do, but all I want to do is lie down. I quickly shake that thought from my head. I don't have time to relax. I need to work. Turning, I glance down at the ice and spot Topher skating. He glides over the ice at the perfect speed. He seems so carefree and relaxed, almost like he's having fun. Topher is typically brooding and quiet, but when it's just him and the ice, he becomes a different person. Or maybe he becomes who he truly is.

Before I realize what I'm doing, I'm leaving my office and heading down to the rink. The team has the week off before they have to get back to training. The arena is pretty quiet, and I miss the chaos of having the guys around.

He seems to sense my presence as I stand along the boards of the rink, watching him skate.

"Hello, stranger," Topher greets me, across the rink.

"Hey," I offer.

I hate how uncomfortable this is. Before Las Vegas, we never had issues talking or working. Now, it feels like I've only seen him once or twice since then, and I hate it. I miss what we had. My stomach churns, and I can feel beads of sweat lining my forehead. Maybe I am coming down with something after all.

Topher skates over to the wall, and when he gets near, I see his eyes go wide, concern etched across his features. "What's wrong?" he asks.

"Nothing. I think I have food poisoning or something," I say, trying to be nonchalant like I don't feel like death warmed over right now.

"You sure? Maybe you need to go rest," he offers. "Is that why you came down here?"

Shaking my head, I remember why I ventured down here. "Sorry, I came down here to talk to you about your new endorsement deal. I will be working with you on the commercial next week," I tell him.

I see his face light up briefly. "I didn't think it would be you working with me," he states.

Guilt creeps up, and I have to look away for a moment. "Jodie assigned me," I say too sharply.

Topher chuckles. "Figures. Well, it will be nice getting to work with you again. Seems like we are just two ships passing in the night." I hate how bothered I am by this. He's right, though. Nothing is the same anymore.

Realizing I need to get back to work and, more importantly, sit down, I push off the wall. "Well, I will email you the schedule, and we will talk soon," I say, moving to leave.

Topher just nods and returns to skating. My heart feels heavy as I walk away.

***

The next afternoon, I'm working from home.

After waking up and vomiting, I called Jodie letting her know that I was sick. A call from Ashlynn startled me as I read through the endorsement deal contracts.

"Hey," Ashlynn greets me.

"Hey," I answer, trying to sound cheerful.

"I tried to find you at the office today, but Jodie said you were working from home sick. I hope you are ok," she says sweetly.

I'm sitting on my living room couch with the television muted in the background as a rerun of *The Bachelor* plays. My laptop is sitting on my lap, and I lean against the fluffy cushions as I allow myself a short break.

"Yeah, I'm working from home. I think I have a stomach bug. I have been getting sick in the mornings and afternoons," I admit. "So, what's up?"

"Wow, if I didn't know any better, I'd think you were pregnant," she laughs. "I had a friend who got knocked up and had terrible morning sickness," she says, and I can hear her cringing. "Anyway, I'm calling because Jodie asked if I wanted to work with you on the endorsement deal for Topher. I'd love to help in any way I can. You were so helpful to me when I first started at the company. I thought we could get some local media and radio stations to attend the commercial. Get the hype going," she rattles on, but I stop listening.

Pregnant.

Morning sickness.

Those words keep playing in my head as anxiety mounts. There is no way I could be pregnant. I almost laughed out loud at the thought. I hadn't had sex since...

Oh, shit.

I start thinking back to that night in Vegas. That was over a month ago. I started feeling sick a week ago. No, that can't be right. Did we use protection? My mouth falls open, and I can feel a panic attack coming on. I can barely recall that night. We were so drunk. I doubt we used a condom. How could I be so stupid!?

"Hello, Sawyer. Are you still there?" Ashlynn's voice cuts through my own personal hell.

"Oh yeah, sorry. Listen, I need to go, but email any thoughts you have, and I will call you back," I say, hanging up before she can respond.

I drop my phone onto the couch beside me. My breathing becomes erratic, and my hands shake. No, no, no. I have to take a pregnancy test. There is no way I can just sit here and freak out unless I know for sure.

***

Twenty minutes later, I'm back from the drugstore around the corner from my apartment, holding three pregnancy tests.

My eyes are glued to each one I set on the bathroom vanity after following the instructions in the package. Holding my breath, I close my eyes and set the timer on my phone. When that alarm goes off, I will have an answer.

"You are just being paranoid," I tell myself.

Gripping the black granite counter, I hold myself up. Moments like this are when you should have a partner, a loving mother, or a friend by your side. I'm alone, standing in my bathroom, praying that I haven't just ruined my life.

When the alarm wails, my stomach is in knots. Slowly opening my eyes, I look down at each test.

Pregnant.

All three display positive pregnancy signs. My legs shake, and my body feels like it's about to give out. My legs collapse, and I slide onto the cold tile floor. A sob wracks my body as I realize what all of this means.

Everything I've worked so hard to achieve will be lost to a world of diapers, crying babies, and no sleep. I don't have a family here to help me. I hardly have any friends. And Topher just landed his dream job as head coach. That comes with traveling and late hours. He won't want, or have time for, a baby.

With tears streaking down my face, I picked myself up off the floor and stumbled back into the living room. Grabbing my phone, I do the last thing I want to do, but I know I have to.

I text Topher.

Chapter 8

Topher

Sawyer: I need to talk to you.

Rubbing the sleep from my eyes, I roll over and see the text from Sawyer. Instantly, I'm on high alert. Sawyer hasn't been texting me since we got back from Vegas. Seeing that she wants to talk to me doesn't make me feel too hopeful that it is a good thing.

I know we have the party coming up on Friday and the commercial next week, but she's been communicating with me via email or through Ashlynn. This doesn't sit well with me.

Me: I will be at the arena around nine this morning.

I type out the words and roll out of bed. It's already eight, and my alarm is set to go off any minute. Quickly showering, I dress in khaki pants and my new Sunnyvale Coach's polo. It feels good being the head coach now. Coach Carl and I have been talking each day as he prepares me to take over. I knew this day would come for me. I just never dreamed it would be so soon.

Sawyer: OK.

She responds, and I look at the terse reply. Unsettled, I walk out of my bedroom and head into the kitchen where I grab a granola bar and coffee, I glance at the boxes still lining my hallway. When I got the assistant coaching job last year, I purchased a small house in Sunnyvale. The second floor has a killer view of the ocean. It's not a huge house, but it's the first house I've ever lived in, and it's all mine. Sadly, I haven't had any time to unpack or decorate, but one day, I will get around to it.

Jumping in my Jeep, I drive the short distance from my house to the Hawks arena. That's another perk of my new house: I live close to where I work.

Once I arrive, I park and head into the arena. I should get to the locker room and meet with the trainers, but instead, I head straight up to Sawyer's office on the third floor. Something feels off as I step onto the third floor from the elevator.

Walking down the hallway, I wave to Jodie as she passes me, talking a million miles a minute on her cell phone.

When I reach Sawyer's office, I stop dead in my tracks. Standing and staring down at the arena, I get a glimpse of her side profile. She's biting her lip in worry. Usually, she would look sexy as hell, biting her lip like that, but the way her eyes are downcast, and her body slumped, she appears sad. I watch her for a moment, before knocking on the open door.

She turns and spots me, and I'm almost knocked to the ground by what I see staring back at me: red-rimmed eyes and a pale face. She goes to smile, but I see past her facade.

"Can you close the door?" she asks. Her voice breaks, and it takes everything I have not to go straight to her and pull her into my arms.

"What's wrong?" I ask, closing the office door.

The office's fluorescent lights cast a harsh glow on the myriad of images and artwork displayed in her office.

"Topher," she began, her voice steadying against the tremor of emotions. She fidgets with her hands, and I see her legs shaking.

I walk closer to her. "Sawyer, you are scaring me. Please tell me what is wrong. Can I call someone to help you?" I don't know what to say to her, but I can't stand seeing her like this.

She blows out a deep breath. "I wish someone could help me with this," she whispers.

"I don't understand," I begin, shaking my head.

"I'm pregnant," she cries out. Covering her face with her hands, I hear the sobs as they begin to shake her small frame.

My eyes widen, and I feel the color draining from my face. I feel as if I was just blindsided by an unexpected check and had the breath knocked out of me. "Pregnant?"

"Yes." Her lips quivered, and she clutched the edge of the desk for support.

It takes a moment for her words to register in my brain. When they finally do, I realize that she's telling me because the baby must be mine.

"From... that night?" My voice is barely a whisper. My head begins to spin as the weight of what she just said falls on me.

"From that night," she confirmed, her gaze fixed on the black and white tiles of the floor. "I swear, Topher, I haven't been with anyone else. We can do a paternity test if you want."

Never in my wildest dreams did I expect her to say that she was pregnant. Sure, we had been drunk and careless, but was I that careless? I don't need her to have a paternity test done. I trust Sawyer and know that if she says the baby is mine, then there is no doubt in my mind that it isn't.

"Are you sure? I mean, that you are pregnant. Did you take a pregnancy test?" I ask though I feel like I already know the answer by how she is reacting.

She nods her head. "Yes, I took three."

Pregnant. Sawyer is pregnant.

I'm going to be a dad.

That thought should send me running for the hills or spiraling into a chaotic mess, but it doesn't. Instead, my heart flutters, and the dread I felt consumed with on the way over here is gone.

"Okay," I finally breathed. "We'll figure this out. Together. I trust you and know that if you say I'm the father, then I am."

She removes her hands from her face and looks my way. This time, I can't stop myself. I crossed the room and grabbed her arms, pulling her to me. Wrapping my arms around her, I do my best to soothe her. I can feel her body shaking, and it breaks my fucking heart.

"Thank you for believing me," she quips.

"Sawyer, I would never doubt anything you tell me." And it's the truth. "Does anyone else know?" I ask.

"No. I don't want to tell anyone just yet. I need to wrap my head around this," she says.

"Okay, I will be here every step of the way. We will do this however you feel most comfortable."

"Topher, I—" Sawyer's words are tangled with a sob, the reality of it all crashing into her like a rogue wave.

"Hey," I interrupted gently, allowing her to cry into my shirt. I need her to know that I'm here for her. No matter what, she doesn't have to be scared. "I'm here. We're in this together. Whatever you need."

Glancing up at me, those blue eyes leave me speechless. "Topher, you don't understand. I don't have any family to help me. I live in a one-bedroom apartment. I have a great job, and this baby will…"

Cutting her off, I wipe a tear from her cheek. "This baby will be loved and taken care of. I don't have a family either, well, besides the guys, but you aren't going to be alone in this. You will have me every step of the way." I see her eyes watching me. She's trying to decipher if I'm being honest.

I am.

"You have a busy job and will be traveling. A baby will be difficult to handle," she argues.

"Are you thinking of terminating the pregnancy?" I ask, unlinking her from my arms. I take a step back, bracing myself for her answer. I would never give up a baby. I respect her body, and I know, ultimately, it's her choice, but I would raise that baby myself before I would ever consider the alternative.

As crazy as it seems, this news isn't terrible. Sure, a baby will complicate things, but a baby is also a miracle. I never had parents that loved me. Secretly, I've always thought about being a dad. Watching out for Tripp, Jace, and Logan always made me feel like I could be that type of security for my own kid one day. Give someone else the life I never had.

Sawyer sighs. "No, I don't think I could ever do that. Look, I know I just dropped a huge bomb on you, but I thought you should know. I'm not asking you to help me or be part of this baby's life in any way. I thought you had the right to know."

"If you think I would ever walk away from you or this baby, then you need to rethink that. Sawyer, I know you are scared and might think this is a mistake, but I don't. Maybe this is our chance to try and have a relationship," I plead.

I feel like a broken record having this same conversation again, but I can't help but feel like fate is giving us a sign.

"Topher, in another world, that would be amazing, but right now, my focus has to be on my career and, figuring out how to raise a baby. Besides, wouldn't we be doing things backward?" she asks, finally offering a slight smile.

"Who cares," I almost shout.

Before she responds, the ruckus from the ice below crescendos, rising to the third floor.

Shit. I rub my jaw as I glance over her shoulder to the windows overlooking the arena and spot the team stepping onto the ice. I'm already late for practice.

"Coach!" one of them called out, oblivious to the gravity of the moment unfolding within the confines of Sawyer's office.

"Look, I have to get to practice. We need to talk about this," I say, reaching out a hand and gently rubbing her arm.

"I understand. I need to get to work, too," she says, doing her best to wipe the rest of the tears out of her eyes. I see her trying to morph back into the professional woman I know. But, deep down, I see the scared and sad mom-to-be. "Go," she urged, managing a weak smile. "They need you."

I'm torn between my duty on the ice and staying to figure this out with Sawyer. As I go to leave her office, I open the door and hesitate. "Meet me at my house tonight so we can talk." Closing the door, I don't give her a chance to argue or say no.

Chapter 9

SAWYER

Sitting in my car, I stare at the house in front of me.

It's a cute bungalow on a quiet street. This is not what I expected when Topher sent me his address earlier today. The outside is white with black shutters and a wooden arch porch. I've driven past his house four times, too afraid to park and face what's inside.

Topher: You ever going to come inside, or do I need to come out to you?

I see the text from Topher, and it makes me chuckle. Taking a deep breath, I remove myself from my car and walk up to his house. Opening the door, Topher greets me, wearing a pair of gray sweatpants and a black Sunnyvale Hawks t-shirt. He looks so hot, and I feel terrible as I glance down at my black leggings and gray t-shirt. I opted for comfort, but I know I don't look as good as he does in comfortable clothes.

"Hi," I say sheepishly.

Topher leads me into the house, and instantly, I'm greeted with stark white walls and moving boxes.

"Are you moving in or out?" I ask, taking it all in.

Topher laughs as he leads me into the open concept living room area and kitchen. "I guess I'm still moving in. I just haven't had time to unpack."

If he can't find time to unpack, how is he going to find time to be a dad?

"Well, it's a nice house," I offer.

We sit on the worn couch, and for a moment, an awkward silence settles between us. Finally, Topher speaks up. "Ok, let's talk," he begins. "We will need to schedule a doctor's appointment to confirm the pregnancy," he says seriously.

This isn't the typical Topher I know. He sounds so robotic and cold that it causes me to shiver.

I folded my hands in my lap, making eye contact with him. "Yes, I called this afternoon. My appointment is Thursday morning. I haven't told Jodie anything yet," I say nervously.

"I haven't said anything," he confirmed. I knew he wouldn't. Topher is a stand-up guy.

"What time is your appointment? Send me the information, and I will be there," he adds.

"About that," I interrupt. "You don't need to go with me. I will keep you updated on any developments if you want." I don't want him to feel obligated to do anything. He can be as much involved or not as he wants. Neither of us planned this.

Releasing a loud grunt, Topher stands and paces the floor in front of me. Running a hand through his hair, he throws his hands up in the air. "Sawyer, will you stop being so stubborn!"

I'm taken aback by his outburst. "What are you talking about?"

He turns and faces me, and his eyes look tired. "Don't tell me I don't need to go to doctor appointments. This is my baby, too. Planned or not, I want to be there for you and the baby."

Sometimes, I wish he weren't such a stand-up guy. This would be so much easier if he could just be a jerk or selfish. Instead, he's caring, nothing at all like Todd. He would have either wanted me to get rid of the baby or left me.

"I'm sorry," I mutter. "I don't know what I'm supposed to do or say. This is scary," I admit.

He stops pacing and hangs his head. "I know it's scary. But you aren't in this alone, and I want you to know that," he reassures me. "Besides, I've practically raised Tripp, Logan, and Jace since they were kids. If I can keep those guys alive and out of trouble, then raising a baby should be a piece of cake."

"I know. You are taking this so well. I've been a disaster," I lightly chuckle. "Plus, I guess you have those guys to show how good of a dad you will be."

Topher moves and sits next to me on the couch. His leg bumps mine, and electricity courses through me. Our chemistry is strong; there is no denying that.

"Don't get me wrong, I didn't sleep at all last night. But we will figure it out. So, how do you feel?" he questions.

"My stomach has been a mess, and I'm exhausted, but other than that, I'm okay. I just can't believe I'm pregnant," I say, laughing to myself because nothing about this is funny.

"It was a surprise to me, too, but since we are married, I guess it was next in line," Topher says, trying to look serious.

I swat at him, thankful for his playful banter. It's helping to ease my anxiety.

"About that. When does your lawyer think he can get the paperwork ready for the annulment?" I ask. How on earth did I forget that we were married!? Oh yeah, the surprise pregnancy really shook me up.

"Don't worry, he's working on it," he states, his body suddenly tense.

"Good. I don't know how we are going to tell everyone about the pregnancy. That is enough for people to try to understand. Imagine adding in a surprise marriage, too." I bit my lip in worry.

"Eventually, people will find out. About the baby, I mean," he says, glancing down at my stomach.

I'm fit and have always eaten healthy, but I realize my body is going to change. Once I begin to show, I will have to tell everyone the truth, which causes my heart to race again.

"Hey, are you hungry?"

Just as he asks, my stomach growls. I've been so busy with morning sickness and work that I haven't been keeping up with my normal eating habits. I need to focus more on that since I'm eating for two.

Grabbing my stomach, I smile. "Sure, we could eat."

***

Topher drives us to downtown Sunnyvale.

The top is down on his Jeep, and the wind blows through my hair as we pass by the ocean. Music plays from the speakers, and if we weren't worrying about baby drama, this would be a nice drive.

"Do you like tacos?" Topher asks, turning down a song from Five Finger Death Punch.

"Yeah, there's this small taco stand near..."

Before I can finish, Topher jumps in and says, "The Sunnyvale Bookstore."

We laugh as we realize we are talking about the same place. Topher drives to a small parking lot near the campus bookstore. Across the street near the beach is a neon green and orange stand with a large sign that reads: Juan's Tacos. They have the best street tacos I've ever had. Sometimes, I go for an evening run, stop there for dinner, then finish my run on the beach. My apartment is right off campus. It's a small one-bedroom on the fourth floor, nothing fancy, and has no elevator, but it's mine, and has served its purpose. Now, though, I wonder how I'm going to fit a crib and other items needed for a baby inside the small space.

Topher opens my door while I'm lost in thought. We walk across the lot to the stand, and we order tacos. We find an empty picnic table overlooking the beach and sit to eat. We chat about last season's wins for the Hawks and the commercial shoot planned for next week. It's nice sitting here with him, having a conversation like old times. When we are finished eating, Topher throws our garbage away, and we move toward the parking lot, but at the last second, Topher surprises me when he leads us toward the beach instead.

At first, I hesitate. I really am tired. And now that I have my belly full, I'm ready to take a nap.

"Come on, let's take a short walk," he offers.

"I really should get home. I have so much work to do," I argue, though it's not very strong.

"Give me fifteen minutes," he pleads, giving me puppy-dog eyes. "You work harder than anyone else I've ever met. You need to relax now more than before," he reminds me.

"Fine." As I admit defeat, Topher offers me a huge grin.

Staring out at the magnificent ocean, I realize it's been ages since I last took the time to enjoy the beach. Sure, I take a run by the shore, but I never stopped to appreciate it. I guess that's sort of my life. All I do is work—constantly on the move and never taking a moment to breathe. And the one time I did, I ended up pregnant and married.

The tide seemed to be whispering secrets as Topher and I walked side-by-side along the water's edge where it met the golden sand. We passed a high school volleyball team practicing, then watched as a few seagulls swooped low into the water, coming up with small fish feasts. The vibe was so calming and inviting that I felt my body relax.

"Hey," Topher's voice broke through the sound of the water, "about that event on Friday. What do you say about going together?" He doesn't look at me but out at the water.

"Like as a date?" I ask, watching the sand disappear between my toes.

"Do you want it to be a date?" he asks, still gazing out over the water. His tanned skin seems to glisten under the fading evening sunlight. He's almost glowing.

"Let's keep it simple, no complications—just friends." I nudge his shoulder, trying to find that easy and comfortable banter we used to share.

"Friends," he echoed, a muscle ticking in his jaw, his green eyes reflecting the last glints of the setting sun.

A family ambled past us, laughter bubbling from a small boy chasing the edge of the surf, his parents' hands entwined. His smile was infectious, and I couldn't help but giggle at his amusement over the waves chasing him.

"Looks nice, doesn't it?" Topher asks, taking me off-guard.

"Yeah, they look happy," I admit.

He kicked at the sand, sending a shell skittering toward the foaming waves. "Maybe someday, right?" he half-joked. "I never had that," he adds, waving toward the family. "I pretty much took care of myself and then took on the guys when I was older. I always thought that one day I would have a family, but I never imagined how it would look."

A deep sadness resonates in my soul. Part of me can't help but feel like I'm responsible for taking that dream away from him. Could Topher and I ever be like that? In love with a little kid running around us? It seems like a faraway fairy tale, one which I can't imagine.

"I didn't have a family either. That's why my career is so important to me. We will be family—this baby will make us a family; it's just going to be less traditional," I offer. Even as I say the words, I call bullshit on myself. Whatever this is between me and Topher right now and our baby, it's never going to be what either of us dreamed of.

"I get it. Dreams look different for everyone. Are you ready to go back to the car now?" Topher asks, stopping and turning us around.

Nodding, I allow him to lead us back toward the taco stand. He's right; dreams do look different, but could my dream have a different vision?

Chapter 10

Sawyer

When Thursday arrives, I'm more anxious than ever.

It had been two days since Topher and I talked at his house, followed by tacos, and our walk on the beach. Now, we have an appointment with an OB/GYN whom I found online to determine whether I am, in fact, pregnant.

Topher: What's your address? I want to drive us to the appointment today.

My phone chimes and the text from Topher should surprise me, but it doesn't. He's been texting me daily, checking on me, and it's really sweet. He's kept his distance at work, not drawing attention to us, but his communication about the baby is sweet/adorable.

Me: I can drive myself. I have to get to work right after

I grab my car keys and purse and go to the front door.

Topher: Fine, but I will bring you breakfast.

Me: Perfect. Thank you!

I meet Topher in the parking lot of the doctor's office, and I already feel my stomach growing queasy.

"Morning," Topher greets me.

"Good morning," I say, swallowing down my nerves.

We walk into the sterile brightness of the doctor's office, and my morning sickness kicks into high gear. Looking at Topher, I motion to my stomach and then my mouth.

"Oh shit, where is the restroom?" Topher yells out in panic mode.

A nurse points to a door down the hall, and I rush inside. When I emerge after vomiting three times, Topher is waiting outside for me.

"Hey, are you okay? I got you some water." He hands me the bottle, and I take a small sip.

After checking in, we sit in the waiting area, and everything begins to spin around me. Happy couples sat around us, quietly talking and eager to start their families. I wondered if they could tell that Topher and I were—whatever we are.

The wait felt like an eternity. When my name was finally called, Topher stood first, offering me his hand. Not wanting to be rude, I placed my hand in his and we followed the nurse.

Once inside the small patient room, the nurse took some of my personal information, gave me a cup to pee in, and told me the doctor would be in shortly. I did as instructed, and then changed into the provided gown while Topher waited outside of the exam room. It might seem ridiculous since we've clearly seen one another naked, but I don't remember any of that.

When I let him back into the room, he sits in a chair while I'm on the exam table. Pictures of the female anatomy and babies hung on the light gray walls. I felt like the room was closing in on me as I sat there. As my breathing grew heavy, I felt a panic attack looming.

"Hey," he murmured, his voice low and calming, "whatever happens, we're in this together, right?" Taking my hand, Topher began to rub circles over the back of my hand. The gentle gesture and his touch seemed to instantly calm me down.

I smiled at him, thanking him for being with me. I know I told him he didn't need to come with me, but I am so happy he did.

"Right." My reply was barely above a whisper, and I wondered if he even heard me over the pounding of my heart.

Just then, the doctor walked in. Her long brown hair was pulled back in a bun, and she had kind eyes that matched her light tone. "Hello, are you Sawyer?" she asked, closing the door behind her. "My name is Dr. Katrina."

"Yes," I answer.

"Is this the father?" Dr. Katrina asks.

Both Topher and I say yes.

Perched on the edge of the paper-covered table, I followed her instructions to prepare for the examination. The crinkle of the paper beneath me seemed too loud in the quiet room. I watched with nervous eyes as the ultrasound tech prepared the machine, fidgeting with my hands.

"Okay, Sawyer, we're just going to take a quick look to confirm your pregnancy," she said, guiding me to lie back as she applied the cold gel to my abdomen. Topher watched but didn't say anything.

As the wand glided across my skin, I watched the screen next to me.

"See that there?" Dr. Katrina pointed at the screen. "That's your baby."

On the monitor, amidst the grey haze, a small, flickering pulse stood out. A heartbeat. It's difficult to describe the feeling that came over me, seeing that tiny little bean on the screen. It was a life. A life growing inside of me.

I never wanted a baby. At least not until that moment. How can you fall in love with something so tiny? But that's what I did. I instantly fell in love with this baby.

"Is that—?" Topher spoke up, his voice rough.

I couldn't speak; my voice was tight with emotion.

"That's the heartbeat," Dr. Katrina confirmed, adjusting the image to give us a clearer view. "And this is the sack where the baby is growing. You are measuring just right to put your conception date to around six weeks ago. Does that sound about right?" she asks.

We both nodded, knowing that was correct. The room was filled with the sound, surprisingly strong and rhythmic, of a strong heartbeat for the baby. Thump-thump. Thump-thump. It was the most beautiful melody I had ever heard.

"Wow," Topher exhaled, a rare smile breaking through his brooding demeanor. His green eyes, usually so intense, softened as he watched the tiny heart beating on the screen. "That's our baby."

"It's really happening," I whispered, tears welling up in my eyes. For the first time since this all happened, these were happy tears, not sad ones. I turned to look at Topher, finding his gaze already focusing on me. There was something different this time in his eyes when he looked at me. I felt it deep in my core. It was something that went beyond friendship, beyond love. It was a shared promise of commitment, of a future together, that was suddenly very real. We were having a baby, and it was right there in front of us.

"Yeah," he whispered back, his voice filled with awe. "It's all becoming real."

Dr. Katrina printed off the ultrasound pictures for us, and we scheduled my next few appointments. She gave us a list of vitamins I needed to begin taking and foods I should avoid.

"Oh, just so you know, sex is perfectly fine and actually recommended for pregnant women, so that's exciting," Dr. Katrina announced, handing me all of the papers and pictures.

All Topher and I could do was share a glance. Sex wasn't on the table for us. Maybe ever again.

As we left the office, I couldn't help but feel different. There was a life growing inside of me, and I knew it would change my life forever. As terrifying as that thought was, I knew I would make this work. Together, we would make this work.

Chapter 11

Topher

That's my baby.

Sitting in my office at the arena, I stared at the ultrasound picture. Sawyer and I divided the images the doctor gave us so we each had a copy. Of all the things I've done in my life, sitting in that room watching my baby's heartbeat felt like the most monumental

"Hey coach, you got a minute?" a voice startles me, and I look up to see Phoenix, a rookie on the team, standing in my doorway.

Quickly putting the image in my desk drawer, I welcome him in.

"Sure, what's up?" I asked, motioning for him to sit down.

I haven't changed anything about Coach Carl's old office. His same old furniture remains. He did take all his personal trophies and family pictures, but other than that, I've only added a few personal touches. I really need to hire a decorator.

"I'm excited to be on the team and wanted to see if there were any extra exercises or routines I could try. I enjoy playing defense." Phoenix is an eager freshman with a killer shot and deadly aim. He's also hot-tempered and stubborn.

He seems to be meshing well with the team, but I think he would benefit from working with some of the older guys. "I think you should schedule a few workouts with Tripp. He's got great skills and endurance and would be a good mentor. I will set it up and send you both emails with a schedule," I explain to him.

Seemingly appeased, Phoenix thanks me and then leaves my office. Left alone again, I pull the picture back out of my drawer. It's hard to tell where the baby is, but I know it's there.

A text vibrates my phone on my desk.

Sawyer: Thank you for breakfast.

When we left the doctor's office, I realized I hadn't given Sawyer her food. Her face had turned green, and she puked, so I wasn't about to shove a muffin in her face. Instead, I waited until I got to the arena and put the food on her desk. She must have just arrived.

Me: You are very welcome. That baby is part of me, too, and I am always hungry! Wanted to make sure it went easy on your stomach.

Sawyer responds with a laughing emoji, and I can't help but smile. It's almost time for our morning workouts, and then I need to meet with the university to review the next season's game schedule. Before becoming a coach, I had no idea how many meetings were involved. I spend most of my time talking about budgets and schedules or reviewing tapes. Sometimes, I miss the old days of just getting out on the ice and playing the game. When I can, I practice with the guys, but it's not the same. When you are the coach, you are the leader. When you are a player, you are part of the team. There's a difference.

***

The sound of my whistle pierced the brisk air of the ice rink, echoing off the walls as I directed the hockey team with a vigor that seemed to electrify the atmosphere. I was on a high, one that no drug could ever match.

"C'mon, push through! I want to see that puck in the net before I can blink!" I shouted as Phoenix and another player raced down the ice.

I had decided to go old-school and put on my skates for today's practice. Feeling like a million bucks, I wanted to be part of the team in any capacity. Skating past the guys, I gave them all a run for their money.

"Man, look at Topher go," Tripp commented from the bench, leaning on his stick and watching with bright eyes.

Jace and Logan were cheering, too. There was a magical quality in the way the four of us played today. It felt like the old days when we were kids, living in a shithole in Los Angeles. We would play hockey and other sports all day and night. It was fun. Today, this isn't work, it's fun. Regardless of whether I have a girl or boy, I want to do this with my kid. I want to enjoy sports and watch them laugh and cheer, just like the guys are doing now.

"Never seen him this pumped," Jace agreed, a grin spreading across his face as he nudged Logan with his elbow.

Logan nodded, his eyes squinting as he observed me working with the guys. "Something's got him fired up. I haven't seen him like this since he signed on with the Hawks."

Yep, something has definitely got me fired up.

Later, after practice, Tripp, Jace, and Logan skip their showers and meet me in my office.

"That was one hell of a practice today," Tripp announces, walking into the office. His excitement was tangible, and I wanted more of it.

"Spill it, Topher," Logan said, crossing his arms. "You're practically buzzing. What gives?"

Usually, players would never speak to a coach like this. The guys have been very respectful of my position, but right now, they are here as my friends, not my players. I move behind my desk, unsure of how to respond. I've never lied to these guys before.

"Is there a new play you're stoked about?" Jace chimed in, his tone light but curious. "Or maybe a woman. Did you finally get you some pussy?"

"What the hell?" I ask, throwing my hands in the air.

"He's got a point. Something is different about you," Logan says, leaning in like he's looking for a sign written on my face.

I chuckled, shaking my head. "No new plays. I'm just... I don't know. Today felt good. The energy, the teamwork, it reminded me of why I love coaching, but more importantly, how much I love the sport."

And a woman who is carrying my baby.

"Seems like more than just a good day on the ice," Tripp prodded, his eyes narrowing playfully. "You're not holding out on us, are you?"

This was it. I've never been a good liar, and the guys know that. They all watch me like hawks, and I gulp nervously.

"Oh shit, there is something!" Jace cheers, jumping up and down like a little kid.

"Let's just say someone reminded me that chasing what you're passionate about is worth the hustle. When you find something you love, you have to go for it. Life is valuable," I spill out.

"That sounds all well and good but cut the shit. Tell us what's going on." Logan crosses his arms over his chest.

Even when I learned I had received the coaching position, I told the guys. Obviously, I had sworn them to secrecy, or I would have kicked all of their asses, but still, I couldn't keep the news from them. Just like this, I know that I have to tell them.

I move around them and close the door to my office. "Listen, I do have news, but you have to swear that none of you will say anything. Not even to your girls," I state.

They all exchange glances and nod. "Out with it," Tripp insists.

Taking a deep breath, I tell the boys the truth. The entire truth. Getting drunk in Las Vegas. Waking up to discover that Sawyer and I had gotten married and hooked up until now, when I learned I'm having a baby. When I'm finished, the room is silent, and I think the guys are stunned.

After a few minutes, I can't handle their silence. "Someone say something."

Fear grips my heart. Are they disappointed in me? Do they think I was careless? I've always put the guys and the team first in everything I do. Now, one selfish night has changed all of that.

"Are you saying you are going to be a dad?" Jace asks, his eyes wide as he is still processing the information.

All I can do is nod in confirmation.

"Hell, I thought I would be the first one to become a dad. You know, 'cause I'm married, and you all aren't," Tripp says, stumbling over his words.

I laugh at his attempt to be serious yet funny.

"This is great," Logan says, pulling me in for a big hug. Suddenly, the guys all surround me, hugging and patting me on the back while offering congratulations.

Their excitement only intensifies my own happiness. I didn't realize how badly I needed their acceptance of this until now.

"I'm relieved you all are so happy. I've been nervous as hell," I laugh.

"Come on, of course, we are happy. We are having a baby!" Logan shouts, pumping his fist in the air.

"We?" I say, cocking an eyebrow.

"Yeah, we. We are a family. That baby is our baby, too!" Logan declares proudly.

In that moment, I find faith that everything will be okay. This baby will have a mom and dad who love them and a family of rowdy hockey players as uncles. This may be the luckiest kid in the world.

Chapter 12

SAWYER

I glide my hands down the silky black gown and stare at myself in my standing mirror. The material hugs my curves nicely. I stare at myself far longer than I should. Soon enough, this dress won't fit anymore. My body won't be lean and tight. Everything is going to change, but for tonight, I must look professional and sexy.

Jodie's words, not my own.

The evening event is to officially announce Topher's spot as head coach while also celebrating the huge Men's Frozen Four Championship title and is a very formal affair. Ever since the Hawks Hockey team blew up in Sunnyvale, the university has treated the players, coaches, and PR department like royalty. Fancy dinners. Charity events. We get to attend some amazing events. Typically, I would love a night just like this. It's a great way to network with people and get my name out there. Tonight though, I just want to show up, stay for an hour, then come home and watch trash television in my sweats.

Jodie sent a car for me tonight, for which I was very grateful. She always did this for her employees and several of the players. She wanted us to enjoy the parties and drink but never wanted to worry about us having sober drivers. Even though I can't drink, it's nice knowing I can relax in the car.

When I arrived, my heels clicked against the polished marble as I entered the grand ballroom of Sunnyvale University. The space was awash with jubilant cheers and lavish decorations, banners of black, teal, and silver draping from the vaulted ceilings to honor the Hawks' momentous victory. A large picture of the team at their Vegas win appears on a large screen, Topher's smiling face proudly displayed with his team. At the center of it all, beneath a glittering chandelier, the newly appointed head coach was being toasted by alumni and athletes alike.

Topher.

"Unbelievable, isn't it?" I muttered under my breath as Jodie walked up to me. My eyes swept over the room, proud of the team's accomplishments.

"It's fantastic. You know, when I first started working here, no one even spoke of the hockey team. Now, they are our highest earners for sports and sponsors," she praises.

"I'm glad to see you up and well. You haven't been feeling the best," she states, eyeing me.

I turn to face her, noting how the royal blue gown she's wearing makes her blue eyes pop.

"I do feel better," I admit. Maybe it's just the clothes and atmosphere, but I'm returning to my usual self.

A waiter walks by, holding a tray with champagne. Jodie takes two glasses. She hands me one, and as I go to take it, I think better and wave it away.

"You don't want a drink?" she asks me.

Shit. What do I say now?

"No, I will have one later," I explain, offering a forced smile.

Jodie gives me a knowing look, and I feel like I'm being reprimanded by a teacher. She takes a sip of her champagne and waves to someone across the room. I am in awe of how she seems to float around like she's on a cloud. She knows everyone, and they know her.

"Enjoy your evening. And, if you need to talk, remember you can always come to me," she whispers, smiling as she places her hand on mine.

It's a simple gesture but also very warm and motherly. I feel my eyes burn, tears threatening to pool. "Thank you," I manage to say.

I watch as Jodie walks away, mingling in the crowd as only she can do. My eyes find a few of the guys from the Hawks hockey team, the Dean of the university, and several of our sponsors. Suddenly, I feel his eyes on me, and as I turn to chase that sensation, I spot him standing next to an empty table.

There will never be anything more glorious than Topher, clad in a tuxedo that seemed tailored just for him. His usual laid-back demeanor is replaced with an air of authority that the formal wear only accentuates, yet his smile remains as warm and familiar as ever.

I wave, and then my heart catches in my throat when he starts to walk my way. Damn, why can't I remember seeing him naked or how mind-blowing the sex must have been? Because, let's face it, a man like Topher wouldn't have anything but phenomenal sex. I need something to fantasize about during my lonely hours.

"Wow, you look stunning," Topher says, closing the distance between us.

The compliment causes my face to heat up and my panties to get wet. "Thank you. You look jaw-dropping, too," I returned the compliment. "Are you enjoying your party?" I ask, motioning around the room.

"It's fine. Big events like this aren't my thing, but I guess I had to attend this one," he muses. "I hate wearing suits like this."

"Well, you really pulled it off," I say, then avert my eyes.

A band at the back of the room begins to play a slow song, and more people join the dance floor in the center of the room. Topher and I stand back, watching as people begin to dance.

"I know that we are friends, and this isn't a date or anything, but would you like to dance?" Topher asks.

He's so nervous that it eases the tension. Maybe I should say no. I don't want to lead Topher on, and I can't let my feelings overtake the rational part of my brain. I just can't seem to say no right now.

"Sure, I'd love to," I say, taking his hand.

We walk together to the dance floor, and Topher places one hand on my hip and takes my hand in his other. We begin moving to the rhythm of a slow, enchanting melody. Tripp walks by us, Sadie on his arm. He winks and nods our way while Topher and I smile their way.

"They are adorable. Young, dumb, and in love," I giggle.

"They are pretty great together," Topher agrees. "Never thought I'd see the day Tripp would fall in love. And now look, he's married." There is a proud look in his eyes.

Topher surprises me by twirling me around, causing my dress to flow and a loud laugh to escape. Dipping me, my head falls back, and when I come upright, his lips are mere inches from mine. I can feel his heavy breath against my cheek, and it takes all my strength not to kiss him. His eyes rake over my mouth, then I watch as they roam from my throat to my boobs.

"You are perfection," he says low and heavy. He places a soft, chaste kiss to my lips. Sparks ignite inside of me, and my heart hammers inside of my chest. The kiss is sensual yet sweet. When he finally pulls back, I'm left breathless.

I'm not sure what to say. Are there any words to say after the best kiss of your life? I don't think so. As we continue to dance, Topher pulls me in closer. My hand rests on his chest, and I want to lean my head against him, close my eyes, and pretend everything is different. Heat creeps up my neck at the thought of what could be between us.

"Sawyer, I want this," Topher whispers in my ear.

"Topher..." I start, only to be silenced by his intense gaze.

"Please don't say anything. Please, just let me enjoy this," he states.

I close my mouth and allow us to finish the dance. When it's over, it takes us a minute to separate. Thankfully, it's time for Topher to head to the stage before the dinner begins.

"Don't leave without saying goodbye," he tells me, as he starts to walk toward the front of the room.

"I will stay until after dinner. Then, I am going home and changing into sweats," I say, smiling at him.

"Text me when you get home so I know you are there safely?"

"Sure."

I watch Topher strut to the front of the room, where he is welcomed by applause. My breath falters while I watch him get everything he ever wanted. I can't help but wonder, will I ever have that chance?

Chapter 13

TOPHER

My phone has been blowing up with texts and memes from the guys.

Even though they haven't told their girls about my new daddy status, that hasn't stopped them from harassing me via texts. Our group chat is about to get blocked.

Logan: Hey Daddy, have fun at your commercial today.

Tripp: Mr. Big Shot might forget about us little guys.

Jace: Make sure to ask for big bucks. Kids are expensive.

Rolling my eyes, I stuff my phone in my pocket, heading onto the set of our commercial, which is the car dealership in Sunnyvale. The owner greets me as Jodie and Sawyer are talking to a guy with a camera.

I know Tripp, Jace, and Logan are used to this kind of attention, but I don't like it. I only agreed to it because Sawyer asked me to do it.

"There he is, the star of the show," Tom Reid, the owner of Reid's Dealership, announces as he spots me in the showroom.

I shake his hand as he starts gushing over last season's statistics. I smile, nod, and respond when necessary. This is why we have a PR team. I am terrible at this small-talk nonsense.

"Topher, we are ready for you," Sawyer calls from across the room.

"Sorry, Mr. Reid. We will catch up in a little while," I say, jogging over to Sawyer.

She looks a little pale but has a smile plastered across her face, so I don't say anything. "Alright, what do you need me to do?" I ask when I reach her.

She takes me by the hand and pulls me behind a large silver truck in the showroom. Our shoes squeak on the white tile floor, and we both laugh. "They are almost ready for you in hair and make-up. I asked them to start on you sooner. You just looked really uncomfortable, so I thought I would save you."

I'm so grateful I could kiss her.

"I owe you," I joke.

The director of the commercial begins barking orders, and a woman starts adding gel to my hair while telling me I need to work on my pores. Sawyer steps back, enjoying this moment far too much, while I am prepared for the commercial. By the time they directed me to stand in front of a bright red Camaro, I'd been plucked and prodded like a voodoo doll.

"Stand in front of the car and unbutton your shirt," the director announces. He has silver hair and a cringy leather jacket.

I do as I'm told, feeling self-conscious about undoing my shirt far enough to show off my six-pack abs. Years of hockey and working out with the guys kept me in good shape.

"Ladies, go stand near Topher, and touch him. Topher, feel free to grab one of these beautiful women," the director shouts as four women in red bikinis prance in front of me.

I stuff my hands in my pockets, unsure of what to do. I'm growing nervous and can't seem to find a way to smile or look relaxed.

"Hey, Topher. You need to smile. You are standing in front of a sexy car with sexy women surrounding you. Show us how you desire and covet this car and the women," the director shouts at me.

How do I convey that when I don't desire any of these things? The only woman I desire is Sawyer, and the only thing I truly covet is a life where I can have a family with her.

My eyes instantly find Sawyer among all the people in the showroom, and a smile crosses over my face.

"Yes, give us more of that look," the director announces, pleased. I'm not sure what I'm doing differently, but I keep my eyes on Sawyer, and they seem happy with that.

When they finally call it a rap, Mr. Reid comes over to me as I am re-buttoning my shirt. "Topher, that was great. To show my appreciation for you and the team, I would like to offer you a beautiful car from my lot. People seeing you drive around with one of my cars will be great publicity!"

"Are you serious?" I ask, completely blown away by this offer.

Jodie hustles to my side. "Topher," she begins, patting my shoulder. "This is a wonderful opportunity, and we will be honored," she accepts for me.

"A young guy like you would look top-notch in this Camaro," Mr. Reid says, pointing to the very car I was just promoting in the commercial. To be honest, all I did was stand there and smile, but you get my point.

As a teenager, I would have killed to be seen in a car like that. However, right now, my priorities are a little different. I spot Sawyer watching me, and I realize I can make a huge gesture right now, proving to Sawyer that I'm going to be a good dad.

"Actually, do you have anything larger? Maybe an SUV?" I ask.

"An SUV?" Jodie laughs nervously beside me. "You're not a soccer mom. You are a hot young coach."

"I think an SUV is more practical. You know, for hauling equipment and things," I argue, still watching Sawyer.

She's pretending not to listen to us, but I know she is.

Jodie eyes me curiously but smiles. "Mr. Reid, Topher has a great idea," she says.

"Fantastic. I will grab the keys to a black SUV with tinted windows and a leather interior. Great car," Mr. Reid says, turning on his heel to walk away.

Suddenly, I hear a woman scream and then chaos reigns all around the showroom. My eyes search for Sawyer, hoping she has an idea of what is going on, but I can't find her.

"Someone call an ambulance," I hear someone else shout.

Then, my heart falls into the pit of my stomach when I see Sawyer lying on the ground, eyes closed and looking lifeless.

Chapter 14

SAWYER

The beeping of a heart monitor roused me from my stupor. Eyelids heavy, I blinked against the sterile white light that flooded the hospital room, the scent of antiseptic hanging in the air. A dull throb pulsed at my temples, and as my vision cleared, I tried to piece together how I'd ended up here. The last thing I remember was watching Topher shoot his commercial.

"Good, you're awake," a voice chimed from somewhere near my bedside. It was crisp and professional, yet not without warmth. I turned toward the source of the words and found a nurse with a clipboard, her eyes scanning over my chart.

"What is going on?" I ask, my voice sounding hoarse.

"You passed out and were brought in immediately," she explained, offering me a reassuring smile. "You're going to be fine. You just need some rest and observation."

"Passed out?" I echoed, the words feeling like puzzle pieces that didn't quite fit.

"Dehydration, it seems," she replied, checking something on her monitor. "Your blood pressure was also very high. We've got you on fluids now. Don't worry, you're in good hands."

"What about the baby?" I asked, my thoughts going directly to the life growing inside of me.

"We had one of our OB/GYNs check out the baby. Everything is fine, but you will need to take it easy. I will let the doctor know you are awake so he can come speak with you." She smiled again before leaving the room.

As reality set in, so did an unexpected wave of relief—then curiosity. My gaze drifted across the room, and that's when I saw him. Topher was slumped awkwardly in a chair, his muscular frame making the piece of hospital furniture look comically inadequate. Even in sleep, his short brown hair seemed to bristle with the same intensity he carried with him on the ice, coaching his team to victory after victory.

"Topher?" I called out, unsure if I wanted to wake him or simply marvel at the fact that he was here—for me.

His green eyes fluttered open, a momentary confusion crossing his face before he focused on me. The corner of his mouth twitched into a half-smile as he straightened up, rubbing the sleep from his eyes. When his eyes met mine, he sat up straight. In a flash, he was by my side.

"How are you feeling?" he asked, pushing a loose strand of hair out of my face.

"Tired," I admitted. "What happened? A nurse said I passed out."

Topher's smile faded, and a look of concern grew. "Apparently, you passed out due to dehydration and high blood pressure. They also asked when the last time you ate was because your blood-sugar levels were very low."

I let my head fall back on the pillow behind me. I tried to think about the last time I ate or even slept soundly. Sighing, I felt guilty for not taking better care of myself. This isn't just about me anymore. I have a life inside of me to consider, too.

"I've been so busy and stressed out lately. I guess I haven't been taking proper care of myself," I admitted.

Topher took my hand in his and forced me to meet his gaze. "Sawyer, you really scared me today. We have to discuss a few things. You can't work all of the time and not consider your body. Now that we've had this scare, I think it's time you tell Jodie about the pregnancy. Maybe you need to take some time off of work," Topher said, narrowing his eyes at me.

If I didn't know better, I would think he was mad at me. His tone was clipped and not warm like it usually is.

Shaking my head, I looked away from him. "Topher, I promise I will do better. I will set alarms on my phone to eat and take my prenatal vitamins. I have to work, though. My career is my life," I argued.

"That's not good enough. I didn't want to have this argument with you, especially in a hospital, but I get a say in this, too. That's my baby inside of you, and I need to know that it's being taken care of." The pained look on his face told me this wasn't easy for him to say.

Sighing, I knew there was no point in me getting angry or lashing out. Yes, it's my body, but he has a point, too. "Topher, I just don't know what to do," I whimpered.

I never liked to feel weak or helpless, but that was exactly what I was feeling in that moment. I was a strong, independent woman who had worked through college and found a career all on her own. I was proud of myself and my achievements. I never relied on anyone for anything. Knowing that I now may have to let Topher in and accept his help—makes me feel gutted.

"That's okay," he said, squeezing my hand. "We can figure all of this out together, but you have to stop acting like you are all alone. I want you to move in with me so I can keep an eye on you and the baby," he said.

Shaking my head, I almost laughed. "Topher, that isn't necessary. I have my own apartment and don't need a babysitter," I argued.

"Your apartment is a one-bedroom. I asked Jodie about it. Also, I hate to tell you, but you do need someone looking out for you. Consider this an option for help with the baby. If it doesn't work out, then you can move back to your apartment."

As I opened my mouth to protest, the door opened, and a doctor walked in. His gray and black peppered hair was full and wavy, and he had a kind smile. "Hello," he greeted us.

Topher released my hand and moved back to the chair across the room. I hated the distance he put between us.

"My name is Dr. Sharp, and I see you are pregnant," he began.

"Yes. The nurse said that the baby was okay," I said, hoping she was correct.

Nodding, he smiled, looking over a chart in his hands. "Yes, everything seems to be okay. I do, however, want to put you on bed rest for the next few weeks. Your lack of care for your body caused you to pass out. This could have been very dangerous," he scolded. He reminded me of what a father would look like when disciplining a child.

"I understand." I accepted his words, even though I didn't like it.

"I will have you check in with your primary OB/GYN in a few weeks to assess how you are doing. Your husband," he said, looking at Topher, "gave me your doctor's information. She will determine when you can resume your normal daily routines. Until then, I want you to rest, eat nutritional meals, and take much better care of yourself. Limit your stress." When he finished, he departed.

"Did you tell him we were married?" I asked once the door closed.

"No, I guess he just assumed we were since I'm here with you," Topher shrugged. "I mean, technically, I still am..."

Again, I wanted to lash out and ask him questions about when our marriage would be terminated, but before I could open my mouth, the door once again opened. I was getting tired of all of the interruptions. It was like fate was trying to shut me up.

To my surprise, Jodie poked her head through the door. "Can I come in?" she asked quietly.

"Yes, I'm awake," I said, waving her to come in. I was absolutely mortified to have my boss and mentor seeing me in this state. I wanted to crawl under the covers and hide.

Jodie walked in and stood next to the bed. She smiled at Topher once before looking back at me. "You really gave me a scare today," she began.

"I know, I'm so sorry. I guess I was just tired and..."

Holding up her hand, Jodie stopped me. "Sawyer, you have always put your work first. I've admired that about you. Your hustle and love for what you do is what made me hire you and keep promoting you. However, it's also going to be the thing that destroys you. I spoke with Topher while you were sleeping. I need you to promise me that you will take some time off work."

I almost shot up out of the bed. "No, I don't need to take time off. The doctor said I just need a few weeks of bed rest. I can work from home," I protested.

"No. You've never taken a vacation. I am standing firm on this. You have to take care of yourself and..." she paused, making eye contact with Topher before continuing. "And you need to think about your baby."

"How did you know?" I asked, my shocked expression causing her to chuckle.

"The morning sickness was the first clue. Then, I cornered Topher when you were sent here by ambulance. He told me what's been going on. I wish you would have told me yourself. I'm not mad. This is a blessing, and I'm so excited for you both. Please, take a few weeks to rest and figure everything out."

"Are you firing me?" I asked, lips shaking, feeling like I would break down at any minute.

This time, Jodie let out a loud laugh that caused her head to fall back. "Of course not. How would I survive without you at the firm? No, I'm giving you a vacation, and then you will get back to work. Whether that's at home or in the office, it doesn't matter right now. Just rest, and please, let Topher help you." She winked at him as she spoke.

"I guess I'm stuck then. No getting out of this," I sighed.

"Nope," Topher interjected. "Hey, Jodie. What do you think about Sawyer moving in with me for a while?" he asked.

My head turned in his direction, and I sneered at him. I couldn't believe he was going to use Jodie to get his way.

"I think that is a fantastic idea. Maybe you two can figure out what's going on with your relationship, too," she mused.

I shook my head. "Why do I feel like everyone is ganging up on me?"

"Because we are, but it's in your best interest," Jodie said, smiling down at me. "I need to get back to the office, but I will call to check on you later."

Once she was gone, I felt like my world had been completely turned upside down.

"So, it's settled. Once you are discharged, we can stop by your apartment, grab a few items, and then head to the house," Topher said, smiling at me.

"You are enjoying this way too much," I deadpanned.

"Yes, I am," he agreed.

Like it or not, I guess I'm about to play house with my husband and baby daddy.

Chapter 15

TOPHER

Sawyer scared the hell out of me.

When I turned and saw her body on the floor, I swear my heart leaped out of my chest. I have never been more terrified in my entire life. I rode in the ambulance with her, though it wasn't an easy task.

At first, the paramedics wouldn't let me go because we weren't family. However, once I told them that Sawyer was my wife and carrying my child, they allowed me to go with her. Honestly, I was going with her whether they liked it or not.

Unfortunately, Jodie overheard me talking with the paramedics and forced me to spill the beans on our secrets. Thankfully, she swore to secrecy just like the guys.

Now, standing in Sawyer's small apartment, I realize there is absolutely no way that she and a baby can live here. It's a nice place with killer views, but it's not practical for a family.

"Do you have everything that you need?" I ask her as she places a large duffle bag on her couch.

"I think so. I grabbed all of my hygiene products and enough clothes for the next few weeks. It helps that I only need to pack leggings and t-shirts." She shrugs.

I know this is hard on her sense of independence, but it's for the best.

"I don't know what I'm going to do with this place while I'm with you. I still have six months left on my lease," she sighs.

"What if I asked Tripp and Sadie if they wanted to rent it while they look for a place?"

Sawyer thinks this over and then finally agrees. "Sure, I think that will be okay."

I text Tripp and let him know. He's pretty psyched about the idea. I scheduled a time later in the week to bring him and Sadie by to show them Sawyer's place. Somehow, that was an easy compromise, and it made me smile.

When we finally get to my house, it's late. Sawyer hadn't been discharged until late in the afternoon. I park my new SUV, thanks to

Reid's Dealership, in my driveway and hop out. Racing around the front, I open Sawyer's door and help her out.

"I'm not fragile. You are acting like I'm going to break," she laughs but still takes my hand as I help her out of the vehicle.

"No, I'm being a gentleman. Don't you know guys are supposed to open your doors? You know, chivalry and all that." I wink and offer a playful smile.

"Well, you are the first guy to do that," she says, closing the door behind her. I stop, and she looks at me. "What?"

Anger builds inside of me. How could she date guys who never thought to open a door for her? This woman is heaven-sent and deserves to be treated like a queen. Something tells me, though. that she doesn't believe that about herself.

"Apparently, you've only dated morons," I quip.

Rolling her eyes, Sawyer agrees.

Once inside the house, I led her to my bedroom. The house has four bedrooms: two downstairs, including the master (my room), and two upstairs. I don't want her walking up and down the stairs since she's on bedrest, and unfortunately, I don't have any furniture in the other rooms.

I set her bag down on my dresser and waved around. "This is all yours."

She shakes her head adamantly. "No way. I can't take your room. I can sleep on your couch."

Hell, no. I will not let that happen.

"No. This isn't an argument you are going to win. Stay in my room. I will be fine on the couch. I've got a television mounted on the wall, so you won't get bored."

"I'm too tired to argue with you," she says, moving to sit on the bed.

I show her the bathroom and then let her know if she needs anything to just yell or text me. I need to do some work on my computer and will be out in the living room if needed. A big yawn escapes her, and I can see just how worn out she is.

I help her into bed, sitting down next to her. "I'm going to put your vitamins on the nightstand. Please, try to relax," I say soothingly.

She glances up at me with hooded eyes. Her plump lips are beckoning me to kiss her. I want so badly to taste her right now. I wish I could remember more vividly what our night was like when we hooked up in Vegas.

Leaning down, I hoover just inches above her face. She smiles up at me. "Topher, why are you being so good to me?" she asks, her voice lazy, and I can see she is close to falling asleep.

If this woman only knew the lengths that I would go to make her happy, it would blow her mind. "Sawyer, you deserve to be treated like the queen you are. Whether you like it or not, I'm going to pamper you and take care of you. Both of you," I say, gently placing my hand on her flat stomach.

Her eyes flutter closed, but not before she places her hand on mine. For a moment, I believe that we are a couple. That we are happy and in love, enjoying a moment thinking of our unborn baby. I allow that feeling to sink in.

I don't leave her alone until she's comfortable in my bed and has the covers pulled up over her body. Once I hear her breathing become even, I slowly creep down the hall to my living room. Having Sawyer here gives me a sense of comfort. I can help watch over her and ensure she and the baby are taken care of. Plus, it might give us more time to build our relationship. I just need to find a way to prove to Sawyer we can have our dreams and a family together.

As I sit down on the couch to work, my phone starts blowing up with texts.

Logan: Ashlynn just told me about Sawyer. Is she ok? How's the baby?

Jace: Dude, you need to call all of us. How is Sawyer? Baby?

Tripp: We are coming over later. Sadie is freaking out about Sawyer.

Sighing, I rub a hand over my face. I'd been so wrapped up with Sawyer today that I forgot to tell the guys about what happened. Of course, Ashlynn would know. She works at the PR firm, too.

Me: Sawyer is fine, baby too. She's going to be staying at my house while she's on bed rest. She's sleeping now, but I will let you all know when you can come over.

I love that the guys and their girlfriends, or wife in Tripp's case, are so worried about Sawyer. I want her to understand that with me, she's getting a huge, ready-made family. She needs all of us whether she likes it or not or even wants to admit it. Taking my time, I work through my emails and even look through some photos sent to me from the commercial shoot today. Starting to feel tired myself, I decided to rest my eyes and take a nap. Before I do, I pad down the hall and check on Sawyer. Thankfully, she's sound asleep. I watch her for a moment, taking in how beautiful she truly is. If I thought I loved her before, that feeling is nothing compared to how I now feel knowing that she is carrying my baby. One day, I will prove to her that I'm the man and daddy she wants in her life.

Chapter 16

Sawyer

Muffled voices float into the room as I slowly open my eyes.

I can't remember the last time I slept so soundly. It takes me a moment to realize that I'm not in my own room. For the next few weeks, I'm rooming with Topher. Don't get me wrong, his house is really nice. Plain but nice. However, I hate feeling like I need to rely on anyone, even when I know that I do.

A light knock on the bedroom door has me sitting up in bed.

"Sawyer, are you up?" Topher asks from the other side of the door.

"Yeah, I'm awake," I answer.

He comes into the room, a sheepish grin on his face. "Hey, the guys wanted to come over to check on you, and..."

Before he can finish, Ashlynn, Sadie, and Skye come barging into the room.

Topher is almost shoved to the side as they rush to the bed. At first, I'm startled and slightly terrified of these three girls talking so fast at me.

"Oh my gosh, Jodie told me you fainted. Are you okay?" Ashlynn asks, sitting down next to me.

"What can we get you?" Sadie asks.

"Are you going to need anything?" Skye questions.

I can barely keep up with them as they make themselves at home beside me. Topher chuckles from the door, mouths 'I'm sorry,' and then walks away.

Traitor.

"Hey, I'm fine. Really," I tell them. "It was just dehydration." I watch their faces, and I can tell they know more than what they are saying. As much as I want to keep this baby a secret, I know that I should just go ahead and tell them. If they don't already know...

"Is there anything we can do to help you? Jodie said you were going to be on vacation," Ashlyn says, patting my hand.

I must look pathetic lying in bed after being rushed to the emergency room. "I'm okay. I will find something to do," I say, smiling. I can tell they want to ask me more. Their prying eyes watch me like a hawk. "Is there something else you want to ask?" I prod.

After sharing looks, Ashlynn finally huffs and comes right out with it. "Sawyer, we feel like there is more going on. No one has said anything, but there is definitely a secret being kept. If you want us to go and stop asking, we will. But if there is something going on and we can help, please let us know. We want to be your friends. Topher means the world to the guys."

This is the moment I have dreaded. I just need to do it—no more hiding.

Fidgeting with my hands, I gather the courage to share my secret. "Please don't be upset. There is something to share. I am pregnant, and it is Topher's baby," I spill out to them.

They all squeal with delight, and Sadie loudly shouts, "I knew it!"

"Why didn't you tell me?" Ashlynn asks. She has been fabulous to work with, and I didn't realize that we had developed a friendship until now. The hurt look on her face tells me she feels like I could have confided in her. I don't have many friends, so it's hard to decipher who you can trust.

"I'm sorry. It was a shock. I didn't want to complicate things at work or bother anyone else with my problems," I replied.

"It's not a burden to share things with friends. Look, I know you are very independent, but having people on your side doesn't make you any less independent." Ashlynn's words settle in my heart. She is right.

"I appreciate all of you supporting us with this. It's nice to know we have people in our corner," I share with them.

"So, are you and Topher together?" Sadie asks.

"No, we are friends," I say way too fast.

"That boy doesn't look at you like a friend," Skye pipes up. "He is so in love with you."

Shaking my head, I can feel my cheeks heating. "We had a drunken night in Vegas, that's all," I say. I go on to explain everything that transpired between us. Even finding out that we are married. Honestly, it feels nice to let all this information out. I've been holding on to it, and it's been eating me alive.

"That doesn't sound like just friends," Ashlynn notes once I finish sharing.

"I have my career to focus on," I try to argue.

"Maybe you should give Topher a chance. See where it goes? You have a baby coming. He's going to be in your life for a long time, one way or another," Skye retorts.

I know they are correct. My heart wants Topher—it always has. But my head has been at war, reminding me that relationships can make you lose sight of your dreams. Maybe, just maybe, I can have both? I have no idea.

Later that evening, after everyone leaves, Topher orders us dinner for a cute little diner in Sunnyvale. called Wave Break Diner. It has a fifties era vibe. I miss going there. When our food arrives, we sit on the bed watching reality television.

"Do you really enjoy this?" Topher asks, as two girls start arguing over a man they are trying to get to know on some tropical island. He takes a bite of his hamburger and then pops a chip into his mouth.

"Yes. Shows like this are so easy to watch when you are working or just wanting some entertainment." I take a bite of my roasted turkey sandwich and smile.

"How about a movie?" Topher asks.

"Sure."

We scroll through Netflix until we find an old 90s comedy. We settled in and watched the movie while eating. At some point, we must have fallen asleep because when I woke hours later, the movie was over, and Topher is lightly snoring next to me. I don't dare wake him. He looks so peaceful and adorable, with his arms crossed over his chest and his head resting on my pillow. As I look at him, my heart seems to leap in my chest. He really is a good man. Hard-working, loving, and protective. I can feel my walls crumbling day by day.

***

An annoying wailing sound wakes me from a deep slumber.

Opening my eyes, I see that the room is pitch black and Topher is still sleeping next to me. He's completely out cold and oblivious to the awful noise coming from his phone. As I start to wake up, I realize it's his phone ringing.

"Topher, someone is calling you," I say loudly, nudging his arm.

He stirs and then sits up, glancing around the dark room with wide eyes.

"What?" he asks, his chest heaving.

Shit, I must have scared the hell out of him.

"Your phone," I say again. "It's ringing."

He begins scrambling around the bed until he finds his phone tangled in the covers. Rubbing the sleep out of his eyes, he glances at the screen and sighs.

"Shit, this can't be good," he says, as he goes to answer the call.

I can hear loud voices on the other end of the class. I turn on my bedside lamp and the light illuminates the room in a soft, golden yellow. I can just make out Topher's face and I see the look of anger and frustration etched in his features.

"Where is Phoenix now?" he asks the person on the phone.

He nods and listens. I watch him carefully, unsure of what is going on. However, I do know that a phone call this late at night is never a good sign. No one calls with good news at two in the morning.

When he ends the call, I wait anxiously to hear what he has to say. Rubbing his jaw, I see how tense he is.

"Is everything ok?" I finally ask.

"One of the rookies almost got arrested tonight," he says, exhaling a heavy breath.

"Who?" I ask.

Unfortunately, it isn't shocking that one of the hockey players is in trouble. Part of job is to help keep their images positive in the media so sponsors will want to work with him. However, there are a few that make it very difficult to manage. At one point, playboy Logan Cohen almost lost his spot with the Hawks for getting into drunken bar fights. Even Tripp had his moments when he let his temper get the best of him.

"Phoenix Westgate," he grumbles. "He was drunk and being rowdy outside of the Wave Breaker Diner. Cops showed up and I guess some of the other guys managed to get Phoenix calmed down. But, it was recorded and is all over social media."

"Jodie is going to kill him," I manage to say. "You know sponsors right now won't touch him. They will think he is too much of a liability with his wild antics to have him represent their brands."

My heart aches as I realize she will have to face this dilemma alone. I absolutely hate not being able to go to work and help out.

"He's such a great player. He can easily go pro in the NHL before he's a senior if he can just keep himself under control." Phoenix shakes his head. "Plus, the owners of the diner are now letting the college kids hang out again. The old management hated having the college kids around. I don't want this issue to stop the rest of Sunnyvale University from being able to eat and hang out there."

"You've dealt with this before," I remind him. I place my hand on his, trying to offer him some type of comfort. Topher isn't just a coach to his players. He is so much more. He mentors them and cares for them. Almost like a father.

That thought causes my heart to flutter. Topher is going to be an incredible father. He already has the ability to help those around him and cares deeply for the people around him.

"I just thought that with this new team, I wouldn't have to deal with things like this. I figured Tripp, Jace, and Logan would have shown them how their actions have consequences." He sighs again and lays back in bed.

"Do you need me to do anything?" I ask. I feel helpless right now. I wish I could do something to help him.

"No, but I appreciate it," he says, squeezing my hand. "I will handle it in the morning. I swear, if Phoenix shows up to practice hungover again, I'm going to bench his ass. I don't care how good he is."

I hear the anger in his voice, but I know that Topher will never give up on one of his players. Just like he isn't giving up on me...

"Well, I don't know about you, but I'm awake now. I doubt I will be able to go back to sleep now," I say, stretching my arms over my head.

"Yeah, waking up like that was an adrenaline rush. Are you hungry?" he asks.

"I'm pregnant, of course I'm hungry," I laugh.

"Why don't I run out and get us some waffles from the Wave Diner? While I'm there, I can talk to the staff and find out exactly what happened with Phoenix." He's already moving to get out of bed before he's done talking.

"That sounds great. I guess I'll just wait right here," I say, slightly laughing.

Chapter 17

SAWYER

"I'm so bored," I whine, throwing down my phone.

It has been a few days since we were awoken in the early morning hours. Thankfully, Topher had dealt with Phoenix and from what Jodie told me, Phoenix is going to make a change.

Sitting in bed, I have gone through social media, binge-watched everything I could find on Netflix and other streaming platforms and bought maternity clothes on Amazon. Being on bed rest truly sucks for someone who is so used to being on the go all of the time.

"I'm hungry and craving waffles," I complain.

Topher beams as he looks at me. "That's easy to fix. I'll order us waffles from the Wave Break Diner." He pauses and acts like he just had a brilliant idea. "You must be having withdrawals. It's been so long since you've had waffles," he jokes.

Just thinking about their waffles as me salivating. It's been my biggest pregnancy craving and the Wave Break Diner has been getting a ton of extra business thanks to my cravings. "Thank you. But that's only a temporary fix. After I eat, I will be bored again," I whine.

"You need to relax," Topher chuckles as he brings me a bottle of water and my vitamins.

Ugh. "I have been, but these white walls are suffocating," I groan.

Topher glances around the room. Rubbing the back of his neck, he turns to me with wide eyes. "I have an idea! I haven't had time to hire a decorator, and I don't know the first thing about buying furniture or decor. Why don't you decorate for me?"

He looks so excited. "I can't go out shopping," I remind him, pointing to the bed.

"You don't need to. You can order anything we need online." Reaching into his wallet, he pulls out a credit card. "Here, take this and buy anything you want."

I accept his card and consider the offer. It would be nice to have something to do. "How many rooms do you have? Can you take me on a tour?" I ask.

Topher helps me out of bed and out of the room. "This is going to be a short tour. You need to get back to bed soon," he declares.

Topher takes me down the hall to the next bedroom, which is smaller, with two large windows looking out into a backyard. "This room would be good as an office or nursery," Topher says, stopping in the doorway. He looks anxious. "It's next to the master bedroom, so we could hear the baby." All I can do is smile.

"Yeah, that's a really good idea." Once we determine the gender of the baby, I can decorate, so for now, I will leave it alone.

Next, we see a half bathroom followed by the living room and kitchen. Topher shows me he only has a few plates and glasses, so I take mental notes of everything he needs. Topher hesitates to take me upstairs, so I tell him that it isn't necessary. There are two bedrooms and a full bathroom. "What is the budget?" I ask.

"I don't have one. I've been saving my money, so there is enough for you to purchase what I need." He also texts me his bank account information so I can keep track of how much I spend. I'm blown away by how much money he has saved over the years. It's another thing to add to the list that makes Topher pretty perfect.

Once we are done, Topher leads me back to the bedroom. He has to go to work, so I'm left alone with a credit card and shopping to do.

***

The next few weeks are spent shopping online and going to doctor appointments. I've missed working terribly, but at least I've had something to keep my mind occupied. The morning sickness seems to be subsiding, so that's another big win!

Once I'm cleared off bed rest, I call Jodie, and she tells me I can start back at the office part-time. I'm not happy about this, but it's better than sitting here all day. So far, I've purchased a navy blue and white comforter set for Topher's bedroom. I added matching curtains and artwork to give the room a manly yet natural feel. I purchased a new black leather couch, matching recliners, and a beautiful oak wood coffee table for the living room. The kitchen table is large and has a rustic farmhouse feel to it. It's probably my favorite piece I've purchased. I imagine Topher and his friends sitting around it, eating pizza, talking, and laughing. I even envision a highchair with a place for me, too.

Topher seems satisfied with everything I've purchased. We go next Monday for the ultrasound to determine the gender of the baby, and I can't believe how excited I am. My stomach is growing, and I can't wear my old pants anymore, except for my leggings. Tomorrow, I go back to work in the office, but only for two days a week.

Topher walks into the bedroom while I'm staring at myself in the mirror. "What are you doing?" he asks.

"I look pregnant," I whine, pulling my dress close to my body so that it clings to my stomach. It's one of those loose-fitting maxi dresses, but it isn't loose on me anymore.

"You are pregnant," Topher chuckles, pointing out the obvious.

"I know, but I'm starting to show now. People at the office will talk." I pull the dress off and hang it back on the hanger. I have on leggings and a sports bra, so I'm not naked.

"Let them talk. Or you could announce it when we walk in tomorrow. I'm pregnant, and this is my baby daddy," he whistles.

I can't help but laugh. I've started seeing a more fun and laid-back side of Topher, and I enjoy it. During the day, he texts me to ensure I'm eating and taking my vitamins. When he gets home in the evenings, we either order food or make something and then sit around watching television. I'm starting to get more energy, so we will start going on walks in the evenings. I'm too afraid to run, even though my doctor said it's perfectly fine.

"I'm being serious, Topher," I scold playfully. "I'm going to look awful."

"You could never look awful. Even pregnant, you are the most beautiful woman I've ever seen," he admires.

I know he's trying to make me feel better, but his words really touch my heart. "You are just saying that to make me feel better," I say, going to leave the bedroom.

Topher stops me, grabbing my hand as I walk past him. "No, I'm saying it because it's the truth. Sawyer, do you know how I feel about you? I'm so fucking in love with you."

His words stop me dead in my tracks. I knew he cared for me, but I've never heard him say he loves me before. This is too much right now. I'm still coming to terms with everything else going on.

"Topher, we need to take it one step at a time," I say, but he shakes his head, stopping me.

"Tell me you don't love me, and I will stop pursuing this right now," he states, meeting my gaze.

I open my mouth, but no words come out. I care for Topher deeply and possibly love him, but how do I tell him I love him but can't have a relationship right now? My mind is full and overwhelmed right now.

He drops my hand and lets me go. "I can't..." but words fail me.

"I'm going to start dinner," Topher says, leaving me standing alone in the hallway.

Chapter 18

Topher

Last night, I gave Sawyer an opportunity to finally tell me how she feels or to leave her alone.

She said nothing.

Fucking nothing.

I know that she's scared and everything going on is a lot for her to handle, but I'm laying my heart on the line and would like an answer from her. I want Sawyer. I want our baby. I want a family with her. But I can't wait forever.

Sawyer walks out of the bedroom, dressed in the same black and white dress she tried on last night, and offers a slight smile. I'm already dressed in khakis and my official Hawks Coach polo. Sawyer had ordered groceries online, so my kitchen is finally full. I've got some blueberry muffins on the counter and a travel mug full of orange juice ready for Sawyer.

"Thank you," she says, grabbing the breakfast I laid out for her.

"Are you ready to go? I thought I would drive us this morning," I offered, hoping that my declaration of love last night didn't ruin things between us.

"Oh, sure, that would be great," she replies.

We drive to the arena and listen to a morning radio talk show.

"Are you ready for today?" I finally ask.

"Yeah. It's been killing me not to get to work. I love my job," she says, then turns her head so she's facing the window.

Sure, she loves her job. But does she love me?

"Well, have a great day. Text me when you are ready to leave today. I'm going to be busy getting the guys ready for a team scrimmage." I don't know why I'm telling her this. Jodie had called the other day and told Sawyer that the university wanted to host a team scrimmage to get fans excited about the upcoming season. It will be a great way to raise some money and invite donors to show appreciation for their contributions.

"Ok, I'm working on the specifics for the scrimmage with Jodie and Ashlynn today," she tells me.

We part ways, and I head straight to the locker room, where I know the guys are getting ready for practice. Even in the off-season, we have conditioning to ensure the guys keep up with their regimens and stay sharp on the ice.

Walking into the loud locker room, I smile. This is what it's all about. Laughing together, banter, and getting hyped up for the sport. Being on a team is far more than just working with a group of people who enjoy the same sport as you. It's about building relationships and molding together to become one.

"Hey guys, can I get your attention?" I call out, causing everyone to quiet down and find seats on benches and chairs.

"What's up, coach daddy?" Jace yells, causing a few of the guys to look at me with curious expressions. It hasn't been formally announced that Sawyer and I are having a baby, but I'm not hiding it either.

I chuckle at this and then begin. "The university wants to host a team scrimmage in a few weeks. This will be a great way to show the Dean we are still as strong as ever and thank our sponsors and donors for their faith in us. I'm going to break everyone up into teams tomorrow, but today, I want to see how the rookies work with the senior players."

The guys seem excited about this scrimmage, and a few have questions. Once we are done in the locker room, they all head out onto the ice for our practice. My new assistant coach is Jax, a guy who won a national title for a team in Phoenix two years in a row. He's a great addition to the team, and I'm excited to have him join us today.

As we practice, I feel that excitement coursing through me once again. Being on the ice with the guys is exhilarating. We split the rest of the afternoon between being on the ice and working out in our training facility. By the time five rolls around, I'm beyond beat. I texted Sawyer, and thankfully, she's ready to leave, too. It sounds crazy, but all I want to do is go home and be with Sawyer all evening. That's what I've been looking forward to all day, and I don't think that will ever go away.

Chapter 19

SAWYER

My first week back at work has been incredible.

However, I'm beyond exhausted and feeling like complete shit.

None of my clothes fit anymore. I'm starving at all hours of the day, and I seem to want naps all of the time. Other than that, though, everything is fine.

Jodie put me to work on the campaign for the upcoming scrimmage. It's been an easy task to get me back into work mode, and it's been fun. At night, Topher and I have been talking about ideas for the game while eating dinner or watching television. Somehow, we've fallen into a comfortable routine, and it's wonderful.

Sadie, Ashlynn, and Skye have also been checking in on me daily with entertaining texts. I never realized how much I needed friends until I had these girls. I hate how I pushed them away at first, but now, I'm happy they are on our team.

Now, as Topher and I sit in my OB/GYN's office for the gender reveal ultrasound, the girls are texting me. They have made bets on whether we are having a girl or a boy.

I'm perched on the edge of the examination table, my legs swinging slightly in an attempt to dispel the nerves knotting in my stomach.

"You ready for this?" Topher asks as I lay on the examination table.

I turned off my phone and handed it to him. "Yes, I'm really nervous, though." I laugh at myself. It's literally a fifty-fifty chance for a girl or boy. I don't know why I am feeling like this.

"It's nice that the girls are texting you," Topher adds, placing my phone in my purse.

"Yeah, they are super excited. Sadie said Tripp has even been looking at houses to buy next year. They want to start a family soon," I tell him.

"Wow, that's a surprise to me. I knew Tripp was looking at a house down the street from mine, but he hadn't mentioned anything about kids. I'm going to ask him about that later," he says.

The door opened, and Topher and I both sat up straighter. As Dr. Katrina walked into the room, I felt my stomach flutter. This was it.

"Hello, it's good to see you again, Sawyer," she says, looking at me. "How are you doing since being released from bed rest?" Her smile is kind and reaches her eyes.

"I've been good. I'm taking it easy, just as you instructed. Plus, Topher watches me like a hawk," I laugh.

She nods, happy with my answer. "Ready to meet your little athlete?" she teased with a knowing smile, her eyes flicking toward Topher. His hand, warm and reassuring, enveloped mine.

"Yes," Topher and I said in unison.

"Let's see who they take after," Topher said, his voice vibrating with contained excitement. There was a hint of his usual seriousness, eclipsed by the anticipation shining in his green eyes.

As the cool gel spread over my belly, I focused on the screen, barely daring to breathe. Then there it was—a tiny, perfect profile. The doctor pointed out a small protruding shape, and the words seemed to echo through the room, "Congratulations, you're having a baby boy."

I turned to look at Topher, searching for any sign of the brooding man I knew so well, the one whose life lessons had been etched into his very muscles as he fought to protect those he cared about on the rink. But all I saw was joy, raw and unguarded.

A baby boy.

Suddenly, my mind began imagining a little boy wearing Sunnyvale Hawks gear skating on his dad's rink. My heart warmed at that thought.

"Wow," he whispered, his voice thick with emotion. A grin split his face, the kind that was rare and worth every second of waiting for. "A boy..."

"Looks like coaching starts early for this one," I joked, trying to match his enthusiasm while my mind whirled with the reality of motherhood, plus balancing the life growing inside me with the career I had fought so hard for.

"First skates before his first steps," Topher quipped, the twinkle in his eye telling me he was only half-joking. "I always hoped I'd have a boy. This kid will have a team of uncles preparing him to be a hockey star," he joked, causing both the doctor and me to laugh.

"Only if he gets his first book before his first puck," I countered. This baby will be loved, and I want him to have a strong work ethic. Something tells me that having Topher and I as parents, this kid will be smart and athletic.

"Deal," he agreed, and at that moment, surrounded by the sterile walls of the doctor's office, we both embraced a future filled with more than just sports or careers, but a family—a team of our own. It was such a foreign feeling for me, but it felt right.

We went over some more information about the baby and then got printed pictures of our ultrasound. Looking at my baby boy made everything feel so much more real.

Walking out to Topher's SUV, he stopped. "Hey, let's go shopping," he suggested.

"What?" I asked, making sure I heard him correctly.

"Yeah, let's go get what we need for the nursery. Now that we know it's a boy, we can decorate." His smile was contagious.

"You want to go shopping? Like at a store?" I'm baffled by this. He's been having me purchase everything online because he didn't have time to shop and hated shopping. Now he wants to go?

"I think it will be fun. We can get everything the baby needs." He is absolutely adorable trying to persuade me.

"Sure, let's go. We can get something to eat while we are out, too," I suggest, earning another smile from Topher.

We ended up going to the mall and a nursery store. After buying a crib, changing table, sports-themed bedding, matching curtains, and wall decor, we found a cute baby store and purchased a few outfits. We followed a saleswoman around with a cart who placed the necessary bottles, glider seat, and various other items in it she claimed we couldn't live without. Once Topher and I were beyond overwhelmed, we loaded the SUV with our purchases and headed to Wave Break Dinner.

As we approached the diner, I stopped and took in the building. The outside was metal and painted a cool teal color. The diner was a small building, but it was a staple in Sunnyvale. The Sunnyvale boardwalk was across the street and sounds of laughter and screams filled the air. I glanced up as the Ferris wheel went around and people screamed on one of the roller coasters.

"Hey, everything ok?" Topher asked, as he noticed I was behind him now.

"Yes, I'm just excited to be back in the real world. I can't wait until I can go to the boardwalk again."

"You aren't dead, just pregnant. Let's take it one day at a time," he chuckled.

He opened the door to the diner, and I could hear music pouring out into the parking lot. I felt like I had been transported into the 50's. Black and white checkered tiles lined the floors and bubble gum pink walls were covered in movie posters and records. I loved the atmosphere in here.

We were taken to a small booth in the back, and I didn't even bother looking over the menu. Once we ordered our waffles, we made small talk about the items we purchased.

By the time we get home, neither one of us feels like unpacking the car. We slip into the bed to watch television, and as we lay there, I quickly realize that Topher and I have unofficially become a couple. We enjoy meals together, sleep in the same bed, and drive to work together. I'm not sure how I missed it, but it's happened.

And I don't hate it.

Chapter 20

TOPHER

I stare at my phone, preparing myself for the chaos that is about to reign once I send the text in our group chat.

Me: So, we had the ultrasound yesterday. It's a boy!

Jace: Are you serious? Congrats man!

Logan: Yes, the next hockey star is on his way!

Tripp: That's awesome!

I laugh out loud as I read over their responses.

"What's so funny?" Sawyer asks, as she sits on the floor of the nursery. She's sorting through everything we purchased yesterday. When we got home from work today, we went straight into decorating mode.

"I just told the guys we are having a boy," I explain.

"Jodie squealed so loud today when I told her I thought she was going to burst my eardrums," Sawyer laughs.

"It's exciting," I admit.

We work together going through everything, and once the crib is built, we are ready for a break. Sawyer has had more energy lately, so she's been cooking us dinner. She moves to the kitchen, and I sit at the bar, watching as she begins making spaghetti. She has wanted to eat Italian food the most for the last few days.

"Do you need my help?" I ask, as she places a hand on her growing belly. I never thought I would find a pregnant woman attractive, but Sawyer is glowing.

"No, I'm just happy that I can finally be up doing things." She begins browning the meat and stirring the sauce while we talk. One thing I've grown to love about Sawyer is her food. She's a fantastic cook.

Once dinner is ready, we sit down and eat.

"I'm going to start gaining weight from all of the pasta we've been having," I chuckled, rubbing my belly. "I may have to add a new workout to my routine."

Sawyer takes our dishes over to the sink. She turns, and I see a seriousness on her face that I don't really like.

"About that. We need to talk about my apartment and the annulment," she begins.

Internally, I cringe. I reached out to my attorney, but I haven't pushed hard to resolve anything. I've been hoping Sawyer would forget about ending the marriage. I know, it's a dick move on my part, but a guy can dream, right?

"Well, Tripp and Sadie seem to enjoy living in your apartment. You said your lease was up soon. Why don't you just stay here, and they can take it over? There's more than enough room for you and the baby here." I watch her face closely, hoping she agrees.

She thinks about this for a moment. "It will be nice to have help when the baby comes. I think it's important that the baby has both of us, at least in the beginning," she says.

I get off my stool and walk over to her. Wrapping my arms around her waist, I pull her into me. "The baby will have both of us forever. I'm not going anywhere," I swear to her.

I see her eyes go round. She stares back at me with a look of longing and, possibly, lust? "Topher, this has been so incredible. I'm just worried that if something goes wrong, we will lose our friendship."

"Nothing is going to go wrong. We have a great time together. Let's see where it goes." I move in and gently place my lips on hers, and this time, she doesn't hesitate but kisses me back.

I could feel the tension within me, like a spring wound tight from years of longing. Our friendship had always been easy, and our attraction was undeniable, but now, it was electric.

The kiss was a spark that lit a wildfire. My hands found her waist, pulling her closer, anchoring her to me as if I could merge our bodies into one seamless being. She wrapped her hands around my neck, fingers tangling in my hair, tugging gently in a rhythm that matched the growing urgency of our kiss.

"God, I've wanted this," I murmured against her mouth, my words a confession torn from deep within my chest.

"Me too," she breathed, her breath hot and heavy.

As the kiss deepened, I could feel her body heat bleeding into mine, seeping through the fabric of our clothes, drawing out a hunger that had been simmering beneath the surface for far too long.

I felt myself harden, desire coiling tightly in my core, born of an instinctive response to her closeness, to the taste of her that was both familiar and achingly new. The need to explore every inch of her, to claim what had been right beside me all along, was overpowering.

"More," I groaned, the word half plea, half demand.

"Patience," she teased, even as she pressed herself closer to me, her hips a subtle promise against mine.

"Never been my strong suit," I admitted, laughter bubbling up through the intensity, a testament to the ease between us that not even this seismic shift could unsettle. "I think Vegas proved that."

Her eyes sparkled with mischief and something deeper. Something that said she was all in, just as I was. I hadn't seen that sparkle in a while, and I vowed to do everything in my power to keep it alive. "I don't want you holding back. Not anymore. I'm tired of fighting this."

"Trust me," I said, my voice low and fervent, "that's how I feel, too."

Our kisses become frantic, and my need to taste and worship her overtakes all of my senses. I picked her up and gently placed her on the kitchen counter. Carefully, I pull her leggings down and can already sense her wetness. I keep kissing her, moving down her neck to the exposed cleavage her t-shirt provides.

I take one finger and begin tracing the outline of her silky panties. Damn, she's so wet. She gasps when one finger slips inside of her, feeling how ready she is for me. Moving her panties out of the way, I slide them down her legs and she helps but pulling them the rest of the way off. As I begin pumping in and out of her, she gasps and lets her head fall back. Her blonde hair dances around her shoulders and falls down her back like waves, and fuck me, if that isn't the best sight in the world.

"Topher, that feels so good," she moans.

My kisses move down her chest to her stomach. I kiss her growing belly, and as I make my way to her core, I glance up to see the heated desire gleaming in her eyes. She wants this as much as I do.

My lips taste her sensitive bud, and I'm gone. As I take her pussy in my mouth, I groan in pleasure at how amazing she tastes. She's sweet, like sugar. Her hands run through my hair as she pushes my face closer to her. My tongue laps at her folds while two fingers continue pumping in and out of her. I can feel her getting close to her release, her thighs growing tense.

"Topher..." she cries out, reaching her climax.

Pulling my fingers out of her, I look up as I wipe her off of my lips. She looks at me with satisfied eyes, and I look at her in awe. I help her off the counter. She pulls her leggings and panties up, and when we make eye contact, we both laugh.

It's a good feeling as I pull her close and hug her.

"Thank you for that," she sighs.

"Anytime." I wink.

Chapter 21

SAWYER

Last night, Topher and I took our relationship to the next level.

Well, I mean a new level. We already broke through our friendship status during a drunken night, but neither of us remembers that. I have no idea what came over me, but I felt myself longing for the man who was working tirelessly to make me happy.

Sitting at my desk, I'm going through emails when Ashlynn and Jodie walk in.

"Hey," I greet them.

They both sit down in the chairs facing my desk, and I can already tell they are up to something.

"How are you?" Ashlynn asks.

"I'm good. Feeling more energized lately," I admit.

"How are you and Topher?" Jodie asks.

At the mention of his name, I begin to blush. Both women coo and get all giddy.

"Oh, she likes him," Ashlynn giggles.

"Of course, I like him. We are taking things slow. Seeing where everything goes," I say, but I pause when I remember how amazing it felt as he went down on me last night.

"Well, we are really happy for you. For both of you," Jodie gushes. "We would like to throw you a baby shower."

"You don't have to do that," I say, feeling loved and grateful for these women.

"We want to. We are so excited for this baby. Have you thought of any names?" Ashlynn asks.

Shaking my head, I feel silly that we haven't talked about that yet. I guess I need to bring it up tonight.

"Not yet, but we are going to talk about it. I would love a baby shower if you are sure it's not too much trouble," I say.

PUCK DADDY

Ashlynn claps like a giddy schoolgirl. "I would be mad if you didn't let us do this. Sadie and Skye want to be part of it, too."

"Can we keep it small? Topher and I don't have any family to invite, and other than you girls, I don't have any friends," I offer, and then instantly feel bad.

"I think something small and intimate sounds," Jodie adds, making me feel better.

We talked for a few more minutes about a baby registry (something I didn't even know I needed) and dates that may work. We decided to have it at Jodie's house a week after the big scrimmage game. Once they leave, I get back to work with a wide smile on my face.

***

Later that afternoon, I made my way down to the arena to share the schedule with Topher for the scrimmage. We included lots of family-friendly activities before the game. The guys all waved to me as I passed them in the hallway.

I found Topher talking with Tripp as I waddled up to him.

"Hey," his voice breaks, husky from shouting strategies across the ice. He leaned against the doorframe of the locker room, green eyes searching my face. "What's up?"

Tripp tells us both goodbye as he leaves.

I hand Topher the schedule, when a sharp kick in my stomach causes me to gasp. Placing a hand on my belly, I realize our little boy is kicking.

"What's wrong?" Topher asks, as I go silent and hold my belly.

"He just kicked," I say in awe.

A wide grin is plastered over his face. Instantly, his hands are on my belly. I feel the baby kick again.

"I think he likes your voice," I say, smiling up at Topher.

He is so happy as he feels our baby kicking. "Hey, little man," Topher coos, talking to my belly.

Tripp stops down the hall and watches us with a smile. Jace and Logan appear, and they watch us.

"Hey, the baby is kicking," Topher yells to them.

The guy's cheer for us, and it's funny how excited they all are.

"Does it hurt?" Topher asks me.

"No, it just feels weird."

"Wow, I can't believe how cool this is. Just think, in a few months, we will get to meet him," Topher admires.

"Yeah, just... It's real, you know?" I replied, my voice unsteady with emotion. My eyes flickered from my stomach and back up to meet his gaze.

This man, who fought his way out of a bad neighborhood to stand as a pillar for those he cared about, now directed that same intensity toward me. He was going to be the best dad ever. Tears spilled from my eyes just thinking about it.

His brow furrowed slightly when he saw me crying.

"Talk to me," he said, his seriousness enveloping me.

"Every kick, every little movement… it's like a tiny hello from our future," I whispered. I never thought I would want this—a family, but I do."

"Does it scare you?" he asked softly, thumb caressing my knuckles.

"It excites me, too." The corners of my mouth lifted in a small, brave smile. I wipe away the tears. "I'm about to be responsible for a whole new life."

"We both are," Topher assured me.

"I know. I'm just happy you are this baby's father."

Topher leaned down and kissed me. If there were any doubts that we were together, we just ended those. This man had somehow broken down all of my walls and made me realize that my dreams can look a little different and that's okay.

Chapter 22

Topher

Life can be very unexpected.

My entire world has been flipped upside down, and it's the best thing that's ever happened to me. Tonight, I'm about to attend our baby shower. I can't even fathom how that is possible. Sitting at my desk, I glance at the small picture frame holding the image of my baby boy.

Last night, Sawyer and I decided on a name: Ethan Cole.

It's all becoming so real right now. He's been kicking up a storm, and I love it when I can put my hands on Sawyer's belly and feel him. He's going to be a wild man, for sure.

"Yo, puck daddy! You ready for tonight?" Logan calls out while he's leaving the locker room.

I give him the finger at the nickname he just gave me. He's been calling me all kinds of silly names that have to do with being a dad. So far, I've heard Big Daddy, Hot Bod Daddy, and Coach Daddy. Although I have to give it to him. Puck Daddy may be my favorite so far.

"Yeah, we are ready," I reply.

Once all of the guys are out of the locker room, I make my way up to the third floor to find Sawyer. When I enter her office, I smile. Standing with her back arched, she's holding her belly as she talks to someone on the phone. Seeing me, she holds up a finger, telling me to wait a minute. I've loved riding to work with her each day. It's given us more time together.

I fall into one of the chairs in her office and notice her shoes are kicked off. I make a mental note to rub her feet later. She's been alternating between dresses and leggings with nice shirts that fall over her belly. She has purchased a few maternity outfits, but mostly, she's sticking with loose clothing.

When she hangs up, she sighs and offers me a smile. "Sorry about that. Your boys are in high demand right now."

"Oh no, is that a good or bad thing?" I ask.

Trust me, with these hockey players, you never know if someone is in trouble or the next campus playboy.

"This time, it's a good thing. Thankfully, we haven't had to do much damage control. Especially since Tripp, Jace, and Logan have found women to keep them in check," she jokes.

"Good. Sometimes a man just needs a good woman," I say, getting up and crossing the room to her. I place my hands on her belly. "How's Ethan?"

Sawyer smiles. "He's been very active today. Don't get upset, but we may have a soccer player on our hands. This baby loves to kick."

"He can play soccer, but hockey is in his blood. Maybe he will play multiple sports," I suggest.

Sawyer rubs her lower back as she shuts down her computer. "Can you grab my shoes? If I bend down, I don't know if I can get back up."

"I'll get them. Good thing you've got me around," I joke. "Let's get out of here and prepare for our baby shower. I have no idea what they have planned, but I told them no cheesy games."

"Good. All I want is to eat lots of food and open presents," Sawyer giggles.

Laughing, I grab her high heels. We leave work together and go home so we can get ready for our baby shower.

***

"Happy Baby Shower!" Jodie announces when Sawyer and I walk into her house.

Jodie lives outside of Sunnyvale in a quaint suburban neighborhood. Her three-story home is nestled on a tree-lined street. It's white with black shutters and a bright red front door.

We walk inside and are instantly standing in a large foyer with a large crystal chandelier. We are led down a marble hallway into a giant living room area. Blue and silver streamers hang from the ceilings and the guys all stand as the girls rush toward Sawyer.

A large table sits to the right with finger foods and sweets. I note they are all of Sawyer's favorite foods and snacks she's been craving lately like orange juice and blueberry muffins. I've made sure she's had them each morning for breakfast. There's also a two-tier cake with teal icing and Ethan's name written on top.

"Wow, this is beautiful," Sawyer gushes, moving to hug Jodie.

"I've waited forever to throw a baby shower. I only have brothers; one has no interest in having children, and his wife agrees, while the other brother is going to be a bachelor forever. You have made my dreams come true!" Jodie grabs Sawyer's hand and leads her over to a comfy chair set up near a fancy-looking recliner.

The guys are watching highlights from our championship game, and I settle into the recliner to watch the game with the guys while Sawyer enjoys her shower.

"I'm glad Jodie decided to allow boys. We get to watch hockey and eat good food," Jace announces, popping a whole cookie into his mouth.

"And, just like you requested, we aren't playing any games," Jodie begins once Sawyer is comfortable in her chair. "We are going to eat, open presents, and just hang out."

"This is beyond perfect," Sawyer says, smiling at everyone in the room.

As the girls begin opening presents, I glance over every so often to notice what we receive. We get a car seat, a rocking glider that the baby can lay in to rock back and forth, and enough clothes that this kid will have a new outfit each day for his first year.

"Man, we looked so good out there," Tripp shouts, watching himself glide down the ice.

Maybe it's a little cocky and arrogant for us to be watching our own games, but we love to check out our highlights and reels. We can appreciate our wins and also take note of plays we need to improve on. Jodie thought I was nuts when I asked if she could play tapes from our last couple of games, but she gave in and agreed.

"Oh my gosh, this is the cutest," I hear Sawyer coo beside me. She's holding up a little Sunnyvale Hawks jersey with my old number (lucky 13) and Lewis, my last name.

"I asked my dad to contact the company that made the team jerseys. He called in a favor to have them make this specifically for you," Ashlynn proudly shares.

My number is retired and is hanging in the arena, but I will happily share my jersey and number with my little man. Sawyer holds the jersey to her chest, and it makes my heart swell. Damn, I love her.

"Look at how those girls are eyeing Topher," Jace chuckles. "Damn, they are eye fucking you." Breaking through the moment, I only turn away from Sawyer when I hear my name.

I see Skye nudge him in the ribs and he's oblivious to what he's just said. "Ow! Why did you do that?" he cries out.

"What the hell?" Skye says. "I love you, but sometimes you are oblivious." She rolls her eyes as he looks around, completely confused.

I glance at Sawyer, who is staring at the screen. I had no idea anyone had been watching me during that game. My focus was solely on the players and what was happening on the ice. There's a strange look on her face, and I can't quite decipher it. She has to know that she's the only woman I want. The only woman I see.

"What else did you get?" I asked, trying to bring the group's attention back to the shower.

Sawyer showed me some cute outfits, bottles, and other items, but I noticed that her body language shifted.

"Hey, are you okay?" I asked her.

"Sure. I'm just drained," she says.

"Let's get you some food," Jodie offers, giving me a look as she rushes to get Sawyer a plate of food. She quickly returns with a plate filled with every item available.

Sawyer thanks her and starts picking at the food while Skye, Ashlynn, and Sadie start looking through all of the items. The girls start chatting about birthing plans and breastfeeding, and I turn my attention back to the guys for a moment.

"Seriously, Topher. That one girl is rubbing all up on you. Why does she look familiar?" Jace says.

I watch the screen, and as the guys are all cheering over their win, a few puck bunnies are talking to several of the players. Two girls are patting me on the back and smiling at me. Hell, I don't even remember them.

"Oh, shit, isn't that one of the girls from that car commercial you did?" Tripp asks, leaning in closer to get a better view.

Skye whips her head toward the guys, giving us all a death glare. "Why don't you all shut up?"

Jace looks like a wounded puppy as Skye lashes out at us. He nods and focuses on the plate of food in his lap. Even Tripp looks down at his phone.

"How about a change of topic?" Logan throws out. "What is everyone doing this summer? Specifically in July?"

We look around at each other and mumble that we have no plans yet. Sawyer begins placing all of the items in some of the empty gift bags. She's been quiet since Jace's comment, and I have never wanted to punch him in the face as badly as I do right now. I love the guy, but sometimes his mouth gets him into trouble.

Ashlynn eyes him nervously. "Maybe we can talk about this another time."

"What's going on?" Sadie questions.

Jodie smirks, crossing her arms across her chest as she sits back and takes us all in. "Watching you guys is like tuning into a reality television show.""Someone spill!" Tripp shouts.

I hear them all, but my focus is still on Sawyer. I scoot closer to her and take her hand in mine. "You know I only see you, right?" I whisper in her ear.

She turns to face me. "I know, but it still stings." She laughs and shakes her head. "I'm being so silly. It must be the pregnancy hormones. I don't know why I'm jealous."

"I like this side of you, but like I said, there's nothing to worry about." Everything else fades away as I stare into her beautiful blue eyes.

"I guess I'm just feeling like a beached whale," she sighs.

"No chance. You are beautiful and sexy as hell," I say, kissing her cheek.

She blushes, and I love that I have that effect on her.

"Seriously, I didn't even know those girls were near me, let alone touching me," I tell her.

"I believe you," she starts. "You were so engrossed in the guys. The girls looked pitiful and a little pathetic throwing themselves at you."

"Hey, tell them it's okay for them to make an announcement at your baby shower," Jace roars, causing me and Sawyer to glance their way. We had completely tuned them out.

"Sure," I say, not certain what's happening right now.

"We are getting married in July. I talked to Coach Carl and got his approval!" Logan says.

My head whips in his direction just as Sadie and Skye squeal with delight.

"Wow, that's awesome!" Tripp says, reaching over and shaking Logan's hand.

The girls get up, including Sawyer who I help, and hug Ashlynn. Even Jodie seems elated over the news.

"I'm sorry Logan announced this at your shower. I didn't want to steal your spotlight," Ashlynn says, looking between me and Sawyer.

"We are happy for you. Plus, we kinda stole Tripp and Sadie's thunder by getting married and pregnant at their wedding," I joked.

The room erupts in laughter, and Tripp flips me off while laughing, too.

"Shit, if we are all making announcements, I guess I should say that Skye and I are going to get married in August," Jace says, shrugging.

"That's how you want to tell them?" Skye admonishes him, but smiles, nonetheless.

Again, the girls all squeal and laugh, hugging and crying to celebrate all of the news. Jodie pulls back and shakes her head. "Damn, you young kids are all getting married. I was in my late twenties when I got married. Enjoy it because this is the best time of your lives."

"Looks like we've got three weddings and a baby to celebrate," Sadie says.

"More like four weddings," Sawyer says, offering me a smile.

As I look around the room at all of the people who came together to celebrate my little family, I feel a happiness I have never felt before. I've got a huge family now. We are growing and getting stronger each day. I love every single person here, and I can't imagine how awesome our lives are going to be.

Chapter 23

SAWYER

We arrive home with a car filled to the brim with baby items.

The evening started out so well. It had a slight hiccup when I became a jealous beast for no reason, but thankfully, it ended with two wedding announcements.

Topher helps me out of the car and into the house. He's still treating me like I will break if he's not with me every step I take, but I've somehow grown to appreciate his overprotectiveness.

When we are inside the house, and Topher has brought in all the gifts, I shower and change into comfy pajamas. Walking into the bedroom,

Topher watches me pull my hair back into a high ponytail to get it off my neck. I've been running hot lately.

"Can we talk about the elephant in the room?" he questions, leaning against the door.

Looking around, I point to myself. "You mean me?" I'm going for humor, but I don't think the joke landed well.

Shaking his head, Topher moves to me and places his hands gently around my face. "You are stunning." Leaning in, he places a soft kiss to my lips, and somehow, it steals my breath. "No, I'm talking about what happened at the baby shower. You got quiet when the guys were talking about the game," he says.

He's alluding to the comment about the women being all over him and how I threw a mini-silent tantrum. This is the last thing I want to talk about right now. I would much rather talk about the degrees of tears during childbirth than how my insecurities are starting to get to me.

I've never really cared too much about my appearance. Don't get me wrong; I know I'm attractive, and run to stay in shape, but I've never felt jealous of other women. At least not until I had a stomach the size of a bowling ball and feet that swelled to double their normal size.

"It was nothing, really," I try to lie, but he sees right through me.

"It wasn't nothing. I don't know what I must do to prove that I only want you. I've always only wanted you." I hear him loud and clear, but it still doesn't change how unsexy I feel. I guess this is something I will have to handle on my own. He's doing all the right things. This is a personal issue.

"Topher, you have been incredible. I swear, I'm over it. It was a moment of silly insecurity." I stare into his eyes, hoping he believes me.

I wrap my arms around his neck and kiss him. My desire to feel wanted and sexy is rushing through me, and I know that Topher can feel it, too. He walks us toward the bed and gently lays me down. In moments, he's ripping his shirt and pants off while I admire his body. I'm breathless as he pulls down my pajama pants to reveal my bare pussy.

"Fuck, Sawyer," he groans, admiring me.

I tug at my shirt, but Topher helps lift it over my head. His lips take one nipple in his mouth as his other hand begins massaging my clit.

"I need you," I breathe. My body is reacting in ways I've never felt before. Maybe it's the pregnancy hormones or the fact I haven't had sex in a while, but I need Topher inside of me. Now.

His erection is huge, and I watch with lust-filled eyes as he centers himself at my core before pumping into me. As he pushes in, I arch my back and sigh as he fills me completely.

"So fucking perfect," Topher says, sucking my nipple before moving in and out of me with a speed that causes my eyes to roll into the back of my head. If our first time together was this good, then my biggest regret of my life would be that I didn't remember that night. Sex with Topher is beyond what I could have imagined.

As we both climb to our release, I feel tears sting my eyes from the pure ecstasy I feel. When I come, I scream his name over and over again. Topher comes after I do and collapses next to me on the bed.

While we lie there, catching our breath, Topher takes my hand. It's such a simple gesture, but I feel the love and connection of our hands touching. Once his breathing evens, I take a moment to admire him before my eyes flutter closed.

Chapter 24

TOPHER

The arena was packed with Sunnyvale Hawks fans, and there wasn't an empty seat in sight.

Jodie, Sawyer, and Ashlynn have done a fantastic job building the hype for our team scrimmage. We never anticipated that an off-season game would bring in so many fans. We've got sponsors and donors packed in here, too. The guys are living their dreams.

The clamor of the crowd swelled around me like a boisterous sea, each wave of sound crashing over the icy arena with palpable excitement. The air buzzed with energy, charged by the collective anticipation of the fans. Their faces were painted in the team's colors of teal, black, and silver, a riotous display of loyalty and spirit.

"Can you believe this turnout?" I marveled; eyes wide as I took in the scene from the stands.

Tripp, Jace, and Logan stand next to me, scanning the arena.

"You led us here. We couldn't have gotten to where we are if it weren't for you," Tripp says, patting me on the shoulder.

"You boys worked hard. Enjoy this because once you go pro, all of this will be a memory," I remind them.

For most of their college hockey careers, the guys have partied and enjoyed the rock-star status they earned from fans and women. It wasn't until recently that they started growing up and appreciating what they have. I just hope they remember these moments.

We spent weeks preparing the guys on their teams and working with PR to ensure the night would be memorable and showcase what the next season for the Hawks was going to hold.

My eyes roamed the glass box at the top of the arena where families sat. When I saw Sawyer standing and cheering, I felt pride swell deep inside me. This is what it's all about—watching your dreams unfold with the people you love surrounding you.

"Alright, folks! Let's get ready to rumble!" the announcer's voice boomed through the loudspeakers, sending a fresh surge of cheers rippling through the stands.

"Remember, no mercy," teased, Joel, my assistant coach with a fake growl as he passed me.

We were having a lot of fun bantering.

"Wouldn't dream of it!" I called back.

"Here we go," I whispered to myself, my heart kicking against my ribs. The whistle pierced through the arena, sharp and clear.

Skates were flying on the ice and sticks clacked in rhythm with the pulsating hearts around me. The puck, like a coveted jewel, zipped across the rink—a prize to be fought for, a symbol of victory in this friendly battle.

"Come on, Teal!" I couldn't help but join in the chorus of encouragement, my voice lost in the collective roar.

"Watch number seventeen," Tripp said, his voice low but intense. He was pointing to Phoenix, a rookie on the silver team, who moved with an almost predatory grace. "That kid's got potential."

Phoenix beamed at the compliment that played loudly over the speakers in the arena. Even though this was a friendly game, it was still a game. We were a team.

As the game picked up speed, so did my heart. This wasn't just about hockey—it was about community, coming together, and the very essence of what made people rally around a common cause.

"Go, go, go!" I saw Sawyer cheering, her hands cupped around her mouth.

"Teal! Teal! Teal!" chanted the crowd in unison.

As the guys sped past me, fighting to win, I couldn't help but smile. I had made it.

Finally.

Chapter 25

SAWYER

The scrimmage wasn't just a game. It was a dance of strategy and will, and as I watched Topher lead his team, I knew this was exactly where he was meant to be. And for reasons I couldn't quite articulate, in that moment, I realized that perhaps this was precisely where I was meant to be, too—by his side, witnessing the transformation of effort into triumph.

I was cheering for everyone because this was a fantastic event. Sadie, Ashlynn, and Skye jumped all around me as we watched our guys do what they loved—playing hockey.

"Go Teal!" I shouted, my voice melding with the cacophony of cheers reverberating through the arena. The final buzzer sounded, a siren song of victory as Topher, coach and former street kid turned hometown hero, pumped his fist in the air. His short brown hair glistened with perspiration under the bright lights, his muscular frame commanding attention behind the bench.

I loved seeing Topher in his element. He was meant to coach. With the help of the girls, I made my way out of our sky box and down to the rink below. I wanted to congratulate Topher and tell him how proud I was.

Both teams were cheering. It didn't matter who won or lost. They were one unit, and their happiness poured out for everyone to see. As I walked to the ice, I saw Topher smiling from ear to ear, reporters surrounding him. Ashlynn held my hand as she made sure rowdy fans didn't bump into me.

"Topher! How does it feel to lead your team to another win?" a reporter's voice cut through the din.

"Unreal! These guys are my family; we fight for every inch together," Topher replied, his green eyes sparkling with the thrill of triumph.

I couldn't help but smile; that was Topher, always serious about his team, always putting them first. But as I approached the edge of the rink, the jubilation in my chest soured into a clenching knot. Topher's arms were casually draped around two girls, their faces alight with excitement as they angled in for a photo.

"Hey, Topher, look this way!" another voice called out, a camera flashing to steal the moment.

"Sure thing!" he said, his grin broadening for the shutter. Reporters jostled for position, firing off questions while sponsors thrust products into his hands, eager for a piece of the action.

"Topher, what's your secret for staying motivated?" one journalist asked, leaning in.

"Hard work and knowing who you're fighting for," he replied without missing a beat, his brooding demeanor softened by the win.

My heart began to sink. That nasty jealousy was stirring again, and I felt my eyes sting. I had to keep my emotions in check. This night isn't about me.

"Hey, are you okay?" Ashlynn asked, seeing my smile fading.

"Yeah, I think I'm just tired," I lied, turning to walk away.

"Wait, aren't you going to talk to Topher? He will want to see you," Ashlynn said, stopping me.

I glanced back, seeing Topher in his element, and I couldn't stand it. I knew he loved me. I loved him, too. But could our love handle everything that came with him being a hot, young head coach? It was perfect when we were together, just the two of us. However, being out in public with the spotlight on him, it feels like I'm alone on the sidelines.

Placing a hand on my belly, I thought about our baby. Would he have to be second to hockey and fame? I couldn't allow that to happen.

Jodie walked up to us, oblivious to my emotional turmoil. "Topher is killing it out there," she admired. "I've already had three sponsors begging to have him pose with their merchandise. The Dean is very happy with how everything is happening with the Hawks," she informed us.

"He looks great out there," I intoned, my eyes moving back to the ice.

Yet, all I could focus on were the girls giggling beside him, their presence igniting an unfamiliar flame of irritation within me. It was ridiculous; Topher was just being Topher, gracious and caring, even amidst the chaos of his newfound fame.

"Topher, give us a winning smile with these beauties!" another camera wielder coaxed, and dutifully, he complied.

"Always a charmer, eh Topher?" one of the sponsors quipped, nudging him playfully.

"Well, if you want a real charmer, meet Phoenix. He is a rookie and rising star," Topher noted, pulling Phoenix over to the cameras.

Turning, I decided I'd had enough. I needed to get out of here.

"I'll see you all on Monday," I said, pushing my way through the crowd.

I could hear Jodie and Ashlynn yelling for me, but I didn't dare stop. I had to hold in my sobs until I was alone. People didn't even bother looking at me as I pushed through the sea of fans. Where was I going?

Should I go back to my old apartment and ask Sadie and Tripp to move out? Should I return to Topher's house and pretend like everything was fine? It was all too much, and I felt my heart beating wildly. My legs began to shake, and I felt another panic attack coming on. I needed to get out of there. As my breathing became ragged, I felt like I was going to collapse.

This was a living nightmare.

"Sawyer," I heard my name being called from behind me, but I couldn't stop moving.

I had no idea where I was going. I just knew I needed to be far away from the scene behind me.

A pain in my stomach forced me to slow down. Then I felt a hand wrap around my arm, stopping me in my tracks. Spinning on my heel, I came face-to-face with Topher.

"Where are you going?" he asked, a little out of breath. "I was yelling for you, and then you ran out of the arena." His eyes widened when he took in my tear-streaked face. "Sawyer, why are you crying?"

Shaking my head, I tried to look away, but he wouldn't allow it. "Topher, I just need to go," I cried.

"No, you aren't going anywhere until you tell me what is wrong. You can't run away, Sawyer," he deadpanned. I felt foolish as I struggled to come up with the right words to say. Placing a finger under my chin, Topher forced me to look up at him.

"Topher, you need to go back and celebrate. This night is for you," I said, sniffling.

"I can't celebrate without you. All of this is for us." He stared at me as though he were trying to read my thoughts.

"I just don't know if I can fit into this world. Those girls…" my words trailed off; he crushed his lips to mine.

"Those girls mean nothing. They came with one of the sponsors and were on me before I knew what was happening. As soon as I realized they were touching me, I slipped away from them, but you were already gone. I swear to you, Sawyer, all I ever want is you. What do I have to do? Tell me?" he begged.

Just like that, standing in the arena hallway, I realized that I was the problem. It wasn't the women, or the attention Topher was receiving. It was my own insecurities. Trauma from a childhood that I had been robbed of. It wasn't fair for me to constantly make Topher question my feelings for him. It wasn't fair for me to run every time something was difficult. I wanted a family with this man, but if I don't start getting my shit together, I'm going to lose everything.

Collapsing into his arms, I couldn't fight any longer. My body, mind, and soul were tired. "Topher, I'm so sorry. You are beyond perfect and have done everything to make me feel cared for. It's me. I just need to get over my issues," I explained.

"What can I do to help?" he asked, pulling me closer to him.

"Nothing. Just keep being you, and I know we will get past this." Kissing him, I let Topher catch me. I allowed myself to be held and loved.

As strong a woman as I am, I am also someone worth loving. I deserve to be with a partner and build a life that doesn't only consist of work. My career is my passion, and I want to reach my dreams, but I also have realized that having someone by your side is just as important.

"I love you, Sawyer. I love Ethan," he says, placing his hand on my belly.

"I love you, too," I respond with a full heart.

Ethan kicks, and Topher and I both laugh. Reaching up, he wipes away my tears.

We finally go back to the rink and join everyone in the fun. Standing among Topher's friends, I take it all in. It will take time for me to fully heal and accept love and friendship, but I'm allowing my walls to crumble. Life isn't worth living if you don't have people you love by your side. This is my new family.

My new dream.

Chapter 26

SAWR

The sterile smell of the hospital mingled with the sharp tang of antiseptic as I was wheeled at breakneck speed through the starkly lit corridors. Topher's hand gripped mine, his muscles taut with protective urgency. "She's about to have a baby!" he barked at every passing nurse, parting the sea of scrubs and white coats like some kind of brooding, brown-hair guardian angel.

The months after the scrimmage game flew by in a blur of events. Topher and I finished decorating the house. I gave up trying to find reasons not to make our relationship work. I also started meeting with a therapist who helped me realize that my dreams could include more than just work and that my past didn't define who I was.

I loved Topher. That didn't make me weak or less independent. It just meant I had my own team on my side. My friendships with Skye, Sadie, Ashlynn, and even Jodie were stronger than ever. These ladies have been by my side, taking me out for girl's nights (early since I'm pregnant) and making me laugh. I've also enjoyed helping Skye and Ashlynn get ready for their weddings. Sadie and Tripp moved into a cute house down the street from ours. Oh, yeah, I also decided to move in with Topher completely. It was our house now. Our home.

Everything was perfect. Life was going easy until my water broke at work.

"She's about to have a baby!" he barked at every passing nurse. I was wheeled at breakneck speed through the starkly lit corridors. Topher's hand gripped mine, his muscles taut with protective urgency.

"Topher, you need to slow down," I tried to argue.

A group of nurses rushed toward us, and everything became a blur as I was moved into the delivery room.

"Okay, okay, we've got this," I panted, trying to focus on the rhythmic beeping of nearby machines rather than the onslaught of contractions seizing my body.

"This hurts!" I screamed.

"Hold my hand," Topher offered.

I took his hand and squeezed as another contraction wracked my body.

"Damn, you are strong. Don't break my hand, babe," Topher wailed.

I glared at him, and he offered a sympathetic smile.

Topher's green eyes locked onto mine, fierce and unwavering. His coaching instincts kicked in as he helped me prepare for the next contraction. "Deep breaths, you hear me? You're strong. You've got this."

As the contractions intensified, so did his encouragement. Each word from Topher was a lifeline, pulling me back when the pain threatened to drag me under. When the nurses finally gave me an epidural, I managed to calm down. Our friends sat in the waiting room, texting Topher every few minutes, demanding updates. Hours seemed to compress into moments until, finally, after pushing for thirty minutes, our baby boy released his first cries out into the world.

Lying back, I caught my breath as the nurse placed Ethan on my chest.

"He's perfect," I whispered, tears spilling over. I cradled our son, marveling at the tiny life we'd created. His small fingers curled around mine, a grip so fierce it belied his fragile appearance.

"Look at that grip. Perfect for holding a hockey stick," Topher admired.

I cried, watching Topher look lovingly down at our son.

Topher leaned over, brushing a tender kiss on my forehead before slipping something cool and metallic onto my finger. I glanced down to see a ring, its stones catching the light, dazzling even in the clinical glow of the delivery room.

"Every wife and baby momma deserves a beautiful ring," he said, his voice rough with emotion. Taken by surprise, I took in the gorgeous diamond ring.

My heart stuttered in my chest, questions swirling in my exhausted mind. "Are we still married?" I asked, searching his face for an answer.

His eyes, usually so serious, now shimmered with something that looked like hope and a future beyond the struggles we'd both known.

Ethan cried in my arms, making me look down at our perfect baby.

"Let me get him cleaned up," a nurse said, gently removing him and taking him to the other side of the room. My eyes tracked her every movement until he was out of sight.

"Topher," I started, my voice a mix of wonder and confusion, "this ring... Are we still married?"

His green eyes met mine, holding my gaze with an intensity that always seemed to see through to my very core. A smile tugged at the corners of his mouth, and he let out a breath that felt like the release of a long-kept secret.

"I never went through with the annulment." His thumb brushed over the back of my hand, a gesture so familiar and yet so fraught with new meaning. "Don't be mad. I just wanted to see if we could make it work before ending it."

I took in his words, letting them swirl around in my mind. Mad? How could I be mad when everything in my life had led to this bewildering, beautiful point?

"And look," he continued, his gaze drifting down to where our baby boy lay, "we made it work." That brooding seriousness that usually clung to him like a second skin had given way to something softer now, a pride that radiated from him like warmth from the sun.

The ring on my finger felt like a promise, a tangible representation of the life we'd built together against all odds. We went from friends to more, from struggle to success, from individuals to a family. It was all there, wrapped up in that simple band of gold and stone.

"Made it work," I echoed, a laugh bubbling up from somewhere deep inside. "We did, didn't we?" The smart, witty part of me wanted to tease him about the dramatic reveal, but the overwhelming wave of love I felt for this man—my husband—washed all else aside.

"Topher," I whispered, my voice steady despite the tears that threatened to fall again, "you're full of surprises."

The nurse brought Ethan back to us once he had been cleaned and wrapped in a warm blanket. "I don't want to interrupt, but I think your baby is ready to see you," the nurse says, placing Ethan in my arms.

Looking into his eyes, I saw our future, unwritten but full of potential, just like the tiny life cradled between us.

Now, I won't gross you out with all of the details of what happens once you have the baby, but just know, I have major respect for all mothers now. After a while, we are moved to another room that larger and contains a nice couch and television.

Finally, our friends were allowed into the delivery room. As they burst through the door, the girls cried as they held Ethan and congratulated us. Even the guys got emotional as they took in Topher with his son.

"Damn, man. I always knew you would be a dad, but seeing it in person makes it so real," Tripp announced, shaking hands with Topher.

"You've always been a dad to us. Now you get to be an amazing dad to this little guy," Logan said, smiling at Ethan.

"We are going to have so much fun teaching this kid all about hockey and how to get girls," Jace chuckled.

"I wonder which one of you will be next," Topher says, watching as all of their faces grow pale.

As I lay there, taking in everyone pouring love into my family, I realized that this is what true happiness is. It may have all started with a crazy night in Vegas, but it ended with something magical and wonderful. Life doesn't always end up the way you imagined. And that's ok. Things change, and sometimes, you just have to roll with it. I wouldn't change anything. I would endure every hardship in my journey to have these amazing people in my life. Sometimes, dreams really do come true.

The End

Epilogue

SAWYER (SIX MONTHS LATER)

It's been six months since Ethan was born.

Six months of exciting new adventures and baby snuggles. I never imagined my life would turn out like this.

Pushing the stroller through crowds of people along the Sunnyvale Boardwalk, Topher and I enjoyed the wonderful weather. The wooden planks of the boardwalk echoed with the cacophony of laughter, chattering seagulls, and the distant crash of waves against the shore. Ethan, snug in his navy blue cocoon, was a quiet observer of the world whirling by. His tiny fingers curled around a soft, stuffed Hawk wearing the Sunnyvale Hawks famous teal, black, and silver colors.

"Look, Ethan," I murmured, pointing toward the horizon where the azure of the sea kissed the sky. "That's the ocean." His wide eyes, reflecting the expanse of endless blue, were filled with infant wonder. It had been six months—six months of sleepless nights and unmeasured joy since he entered our world and anchored our little family with his gummy smiles and infectious giggles. He was the perfect combination of both Topher and myself. He was perfect.

Topher and I were planning on taking a much-needed vacation and couldn't wait to show Ethan the world. We wanted to give him all of the things that we never had as kids.

The late afternoon sun reflected off the ocean, causing little sparks of light to dance along the waves. Though our life had become super hectic since having Ethan, Topher had been incredible. Always the doting father and husband, he constantly vowed to do what he could to make us happy. Like today, he planned a surprise family outing for us. It was simple and sweet and everything I loved about this man. These simple moments, just the three of us, felt like the pieces of a puzzle finally clicking together, the picture of our family now complete. Ethan's presence had woven a new layer into the fabric of our lives.

Sometimes, I felt like fate had brought Ethan into our lives to ensure that two hardheaded people would finally get together.

"I'm so glad you planned this little date today," I sighed, leaning against Topher.

We paused for a moment, allowing the ebb and flow of the crowd to pass as we looked out at the vast ocean. Six months had transformed everything, yet here, on this bustling boardwalk, with the rhythmic lull of the sea, it felt as though time stood still, encapsulating us in its serene bubble. There was nothing but the gentle creak of the stroller, the whisper of the breeze, and the silent promise that whatever the tides brought in, we'd weather it together—as a family, complete and whole.

"Me, too," Topher agreed.

When we weren't working, we were usually surrounded by our friends who had become an extension of our family. They loved Ethan and always wanted to come and spend time with him. Not even a year old, Ethan was spoiled rotten with his constant gifts and cuddles from everyone. Now that Tripp and Sadie were expecting a baby, I knew the others would soon be adding to their families. I loved getting to shop with Sadie for baby clothes. Especially since she's having a little girl.

Don't get me wrong, I adore our friends and cherish every moment with them, but sometimes, I just miss these moments. I think Topher does, too.

"Look at that," he said, pointing to the Ferris wheel that towered above the arcade games and cotton candy stands, its vibrant colors winking in the sunlight.

Ethan looked up, giggling and kicking his chubby little legs at the sigh. Topher and I laughed, watching the excitement grow on his face. His eyes sparkled with child-like excitement, a reflection of the joy I saw in Ethan's wide-eyed gaze when he discovered something new.

"Watch that kid kick. He's going to be playing hockey like a pro before he's in kindergarten," Topher admired.

I never argued. I knew that hockey ran in Ethan's blood. The kid would be on the ice in no time.

"Let's go on it," Topher suggested, his grin contagious.

"Are you sure he's not too small?" I asked, glancing down at Ethan, who was now babbling contentedly, entranced by the sight of seagulls swooping low.

"They have one of those enclosed carriages. We'll be fine," Topher reassured me, already steering us towards the queue.

We nestled into the carriage, the three of us snug against the padded bench seat. Topher's arm wrapped around my shoulders, pulling me a little closer as we began our ascent. Below, the boardwalk became a blur of colors and movement, sounds melding into a distant hum. Ethan's eyes widened in silent awe, and I watched as his tiny hand reached for the sky, as if he could grasp the sun's rays that danced upon his fingers.

"I love how small Sunnyvale is. You can see the entire town from up here," I murmured, leaning into Topher's side.

"It's our home. I don't want to be anywhere else," he replied softly.

After the ride, we continued down the boardwalk. We played games and won Ethan a large dolphin, we ate cotton candy, and watched people who moved around us.

As dusk painted the sky in hues of orange and purple, we moved away from the jangle of arcade games to the quieter end of the boardwalk. We found a bench, the wood was worn smooth by countless visitors before us, and settled there to watch the sun's grand finale. Ethan, now drowsy from the day's excitement, lay sleeping in his stroller. He was surrounded by stuffed animals and his little hands were sticky and covered in pink cotton candy.

Topher slipped an arm around me, and together, we watched as the sun dipped lower, its reflection a fiery path across the water's surface. I leaned into him, feeling the beat of his heart against my side.

"This is perfect," I breathed.

"We need more moments like this. We need to carve more time out as a family. And, we need to add to our family. I need an entire hockey team," he chuckled.

"Let's wait a few more months and then we can try for baby number two. But, let's make sure we remember the conception this time," I giggled.

Nuzzling his nose against my neck, Topher whispered, "I want to remember every moment with you. Now and forever."

My heart swelled inside my chest. I still don't know how I got so lucky to have this unbelievable man by my side. Our relationship sure didn't start perfect, but nothing ever does. I love this life we've created and can't wait to see what our next chapter brings.

Afterword

Want more of Sunnyvale University's hot jocks?

Check out the new team for the Sunnyvale Hawks. This time, we follow playboy, Phoenix in The Fake Out.

The star player for the Sunnyvale Hawks Hockey Team just kissed me in front of an entire party.

Now, he's telling everyone he's my boyfriend.
Sounds great, right?
Problem is, I've never met this man before in my life.
Things just went from awkward to complicated.

After transferring to Sunnyvale University, I was ready for a fresh new start and a new identity. However, what I didn't expect was to see the person who destroyed my life and forced me to transfer schools mid-semester, to be attending Sunnyvale, too. She knows my secrets and has the power to destroy everything I've created for myself. Feeling hopeless, I worry my dream of starting over won't happen.

Everything changes when Phoenix Westgate, the Sunnyvale Hawks star player and notorious playboy kisses me at a party and calls me his girlfriend. Guys like Phoenix don't typically date girls like me. I'm not into parties and I hate being in the spotlight. But with one kiss that went viral on social media, I'm not thrust into his world whether I like it or not.

Now, suddenly people are noticing me my ex-best friend is leaving me alone. This would all be perfect if Phoenix didn't have his own motives. Needing to improve his image with his team and the media, he devises a plan for me to be his fake girlfriend.

As we begin our charade, walls crumble as emotions get mixed into our game. I'm losing sight of what is real and what's fake anymore. Will Phoenix and I get what we want without losing our hearts in the process? Or, will we just have to fake it?

The Fake Out is a spin-off series from the Puck Me: Sunnyvale Hawks Series.

Tropes:

Fake Dating

College Romance

Bully

Friends to Lovers

Grab Your Copy Here!

About the author

M. A. Lee is the persona of a wife, mother, and romance author. When not obsessing over coffee, M. A. Lee loves creating naughty romance novels with book boyfriends that will make you swoon.

Find M. A. Lee on Social Media-

Facebook-MA Lee

Facebook Page - Author MA Lee

Facebook Series Page - Breaking Boundaries Series

Facebook ARC Review Team - MA Lee and Michelle Areaux's ARC Review Team

Facebook Group - Readers of Steamy Romance Novels by M.A. Lee

Twitter - AuthorMALee

Instagram - malee0113

E-mail - malee0113@gmail.com

If you want to sign up for my newsletter, send me an e-mail or complete the newsletter form on my Facebook pages.

Also by

The Breaking Boundaries Series
Breaking Boundaries
Breaking Through
Breaking Promises
Breaking Trust
The Heavy Hitters Series
Knock Out
Stone Cold
A Christmas Anthology
'Tis the Season
New Jersey Boy
Chasing Us
A Savannah Mafia Romance
Cruel Prince
Cruel Warrior
Cruel King
Cruel Knight

**Multi-author collaborations
that can be read as standalone novels.**

The Raven Boys Series

Twin Flames

Burning Hearts

The Crimes of Passion Series

Faded

The Shady Oaks Series

Moonstruck

The Legacy Series

A Shot at Love

Running to You

A Rescue Me Series Novel

Heart to Heart

Blazing for You

Aiming for You

An Everyday Heroes World Novel

Taken

The Driven World Series Novel

Limitless

Rush

A Hero Club Novel

Cocky Professor

Made in the USA
Middletown, DE
11 May 2025